Digging

A Heavenly Highland Inn Cozy Mystery

Cindy Bell

ISBN-13: 978-1535130547

ISBN-10: 1535130547

Table of Contents

Chapter One

The soft trill of a songbird drew Vicky from her sleep. It was nearly spring and the birds were ready for it. The weather was still very cool in the mornings and the evenings, but the days were warming up. As she slowly opened her eyes she felt the warmth of an arm around her. She was still getting used to the sensation. Rather than being startled by it, now she was comforted by it. She remained still for a moment and listened to the sound of Mitchell's steady breath. It was almost a snore, but not quite. Since he had moved in Vicky had found the sound to be very reassuring. She glanced down at her wedding ring for a moment, as she had every morning since they had returned from their honeymoon. Each time she felt like the luckiest woman in the world. She found it amusing now that she had been so hesitant to move forward with Mitchell.

Carefully, she wriggled out from under his arm. He had a late call the night before and she wanted to let him sleep as long as he possibly could. As a married woman she was becoming a little more domestic, or at least attempting to. She started preparing breakfast for them both. She was just putting the plates down on the breakfast bar when she heard the shrill ring of Mitchell's cell phone. She knew that meant he had a case. She hurried to pour him a glass of juice. Mitchell rushed around the bedroom getting dressed. When he stepped out he smiled at Vicky. She loved the way he would suddenly stop whatever he was doing when he looked at her.

"Morning, love." He walked towards her.

"Morning." She leaned across the breakfast bar to kiss him. "Do you have a minute for breakfast or is it an emergency?"

Mitchell looked at the slightly burnt toast, and runny eggs. "Let's put it this way, whatever is going on isn't going to get any worse if I share breakfast with my beautiful wife." He smiled and sat down at the bar. "Thanks for this."

"Don't worry, Chef Henry is going to teach me." Vicky grimaced as she sat down beside him.

"Vicky, I don't care what you prepare, it's always delicious. Besides, you don't have to make me breakfast, or lunch, or dinner, I can manage it on my own." He met her eyes. "You don't have to cater for me."

"I know that." She smiled a little. "Don't let this get public, but I actually enjoy it."

"It'll be our secret." He grinned.

"I just can't wait until the house is built." Vicky glanced towards the window that overlooked the rolling grounds beyond the inn's primary property. She and Mitchell were building a house of their own on the property. All that she could see now was some dirt they had dug up to lay the foundations. Once it was built Vicky's Aunt Ida would get to move into Vicky's apartment. It would all work out just fine once the house was built, and there were less occasions of Ida bursting through the door at the wrong moments.

"It will be nice to have our own home." Mitchell smiled. "I can't wait to carry you over the threshold."

Vicky laughed and shot him a light wink. "You'd better get to the gym then."

"What are you trying to say?" He faked a glare.

"Nothing, sweetie." She kissed his cheek.

"I better get going." Mitchell polished off the last of his breakfast. "Stay out of trouble, hmm?" He raised an eyebrow as he looked at Vicky. "No matter what Aunt Ida tries to get you into."

Vicky smiled mischievously. "Can't make any promises."

Mitchell leaned in for a quick kiss and then headed out the door. Vicky watched him go. Once the door closed behind him she began clearing up the dinner dishes. As she washed them she hummed under her breath. It wasn't often that she had her apartment to herself. She did miss living alone in some ways. But she wouldn't trade Mitchell being there with her for anything.

Within moments of putting the last dry dish in the cabinet, there was a knock on her door. Of course she didn't have the opportunity to answer it before Ida opened it herself and strutted into the apartment. She was dressed in a neon green pants suit that reminded Vicky of a slightly off color highlighter. She had to squint slightly as Ida walked towards her.

"Oh, Vicky I'm so glad that you're home!" She flopped down on the couch. "Do you know who checked in yesterday?"

"Who?"

"Roman Blade," Ida spoke the name as if it was a poem rolling off the tip of her tongue. "He is staying here, under the same roof as us. Isn't that amazing? It's his brief break from the campaign trail."

"Oh, yes I know he checked in with his campaign manager. He's running for senator or mayor right?" Vicky frowned. She didn't follow politics until it was time to vote, at which point she would just ask Sarah who was the most decent candidate and vote accordingly. She trusted her sister, who always kept up on the latest news and politics.

"For governor, Vicky," Ida admonished. "How could you not know that? Haven't you seen his dreamy, brown eyes?"

"Aunt Ida, I'm married." Vicky held up her hand with her wedding ring on it. "No more dreamy, brown eyes for me."

"Oh please, you can still look." Ida smiled. "He's very pleasant to look at. I'm hoping to have the chance to spend some time with him."

"Aunt Ida, no harassing the guests, remember?" Vicky lifted an eyebrow with a hint of warning in her voice.

"Who's harassing?" Ida giggled in a girlish fashion. "I'm just admiring him. He's going to go far you know. It would be best to make a friend out of him. Celebrities already like to stay here, but this could be a chance to break into the political arena. We could host mayors, governors, senators, even the President of the United States!"

"Okay, okay." Vicky laughed. "I think you're getting ahead of yourself." She looked at her aunt with admiration. Ida had her quirky ways, but there was no woman in the world that Vicky looked up to more. She had lived a very adventurous life, and still been selfless enough to sacrifice all of that to take over the parenting role of Vicky and her sister, Sarah, after their parents passed away. She looked twenty years younger than she actually was and acted about forty years younger. Ida didn't understand the concept of holding back.

"All I'm saying is that we need to take our opportunities when they present themselves." Ida cleared her throat. "Here we have a future governor under our roof and no one has even offered to give him a guided tour of this historical property or of Highland."

"It's not that historical. Sarah already took the campaign manager on a tour of the inn and grounds this morning as they were considering holding some campaign events here." Vicky smiled. "But, I suppose it wouldn't hurt to check in on Roman and see if he or his campaign manager need anything. I could do it, but maybe..."

"I would love to! Absolutely! I can't wait!" Ida jumped up from the couch.

"Just remember, Aunt Ida, if he declines, don't try to coerce him. He came here for a little break from the campaign trail, not to be pressured." She met her aunt's eyes with determination.

"Oh fine, it's not like I would abduct him or something. Really, Vicky." She shook her head.

"Remember when that singer stayed here and...?"

"Oh, that was one time, Vicky!" Ida huffed with exasperation and began heading towards the door. "Besides, how was I supposed to know that Mitchell didn't have a spare handcuff key?"

Vicky shook her head and opened the door for her aunt. The moment she did she heard a piercing shriek coming from the banquet hall.

Chapter Two

The sound of the scream made Vicky's heart stop beating, not because of how loud it was, but because of who she knew it was coming from.

"Sarah!" Vicky gasped her sister's name and ran towards the shrieking. Ida ran right behind her. The short hallway between Vicky's apartment and the banquet hall was empty, but the banquet hall doors were flung wide open.

When Vicky ran through the doors she was shocked that her feet squished into soaked carpet. She looked up just in time to be hit in the face by a stream of water.

"Oh!" She cried out in surprise and reached up to shield her face. Ida moved carefully around her and avoided most of the splash. "What is going on?"

Sarah was standing in the middle of a growing puddle in the center of the banquet hall. She was soaked from head to toe, her dress hung soggily from her shoulders.

"Vicky, what are we going to do?" she moaned.

"Turn the water off." Vicky went running for the back door, but as she crossed the puddle her foot slid in the water. She lost her balance and toppled into Sarah, who also slid in the water. They ended up in a pile, with Ida's laughter surrounding them.

"Aunt Ida!" Sarah pouted in her direction. "There is nothing funny about this."

Suddenly the water stopped spraying. It didn't make up for the soaked carpeting or dripping furnishings, but Sarah sighed with relief.

"I'm sorry, girls. Seeing you two in that puddle just reminded me so much of when you used to make mud pies in the backyard. You even left them in the sun to bake. I once took a big bite of dirt just to make you smile, Sarah." Ida giggled. "You were too smart to believe me when I tried to toss it over my shoulder when you weren't looking."

"I remember that." Vicky grinned. "Sarah, you would get so angry if people didn't actually eat it."

"Oh really?" Ida placed her hands on her hips. "I recall that your way of getting people to eat the pies was to fling them in their face, Vicky!"

Vicky gulped and glanced away quickly. "Hmm, I don't remember that."

"I bet you don't." Sarah managed a smile. "But this isn't the time to talk about mud pies. We need to figure out what happened and how to get it cleaned up as fast as possible."

"I wonder who turned the water off?" Vicky looked back up at the ceiling warily as if she expected it to suddenly spray water again.

The side door that led from the banquet hall to the patio beside the pool swung open. Henry, the chef who ran the restaurant for the inn, rushed inside.

"I just turned the water off to the whole building, so we may get a few complaints if any guests were in the middle of showers."

Henry was a little out of breath, his cheeks were red. It was clear that he had moved as fast as possible to stop the flow of water.

"Thank you, Henry!" Sarah said. "I can't believe this happened."

"I saw the water pouring out from outside. What happened?" Henry frowned.

"I have no idea." Sarah peered up at the ceiling. "I'm pretty sure that the sprinkler is broken. I don't know why it went off, or how it could have been broken. We just had an inspection not that long ago. This is a disaster!"

Vicky looked over at Sarah with some concern. She knew that her sister took her role very seriously and that she carried the weight of the inn on her shoulders. Vicky did her best to help out, but her skills were more oriented to party planning and decoration than organization and crisis management.

"It's going to be okay, Sarah. At least there wasn't a real fire." Vicky smiled, hoping to draw her sister into the bright side.

"There might as well have been!" Sarah pressed her foot into the carpet. A fresh pool of water rose up beneath her shoe. "Everything is destroyed."

"We can dry it out." Henry gestured towards the kitchen. "I have some large fans."

"We have more in storage in case the air-conditioner stops working during the summer. I'll send the new bellboy down to get them." The restaurant was closed for painting so Vicky pointed to the patio beyond the glass door. "We can set the nice dining area outside for lunch. We'll just have to add more tables. It's going to be fine, Sarah. We'll get it all worked out."

"I hope so." Sarah frowned. "I don't want to have to lose the money for everyone's stay here, but if we can't provide the meals we offer then we are going to have to think about giving a discount."

"Don't be too hasty with the discounts." Ida waved her hand in the air. "There's no reason people can't eat outside or if they don't like that, they can have their food in their rooms. Problems happen. Now the important thing is how we fix it. Of course, I can't help too much. I have to be a tour guide."

Vicky rolled her eyes at her aunt's ironclad memory. She wasn't going to miss her chance at escorting her political crush around town for anything.

"That's fine, Aunt Ida." Vicky started pulling off the wet tablecloths from nearby tables. "I can handle this. It's probably best if you keep our special guest out of the inn for as long as possible. We don't need a hit to our reputation."

"I think that's a good idea, too." Sarah nodded. "Use whatever you need from petty cash to show him a good time, okay?"

"Oh, Sarah," Vicky mumbled.

"Within reason," Sarah added quickly. She glanced at her watch and winced. "I hate to do this, Vicky, but I have a few more guests due to check in and I need to be at the front desk. Do you think you could get things started in here while I take care of reception?" Sarah looked at her sister with a hint of guilt in her eyes.

"Sure, no problem." Vicky smiled at Sarah. "Just leave it to me. I'll get someone out here to fix the sprinkler as fast as possible so that we can get the water back on. Just do me a favor and send Blake in if you see him. Remember, he started yesterday?"

"Oh, the kid right?" Sarah frowned. "Are you sure about him, Vicky? He seems pretty young."

"Sarah, he's not that young, he's nineteen. We're just getting old." Vicky laughed.

"I guess you're right about that." Sarah sighed. "Thanks, Sis." She walked out of the banquet hall. Vicky tried not to laugh at the way her shoes squished as she walked. Even though the situation was dire, it was still good to find humor in it. Vicky pulled out her cell phone and called the plumber they usually used when anything went wrong at the inn. His phone rang several times before his wife finally answered. Vicky explained the situation quickly.

"I'm sorry, Vicky, Brad's so sick today, he won't be able to make it. You could call his cousin, Benny, he could probably help."

Vicky wondered for a moment what else could go wrong. Then she reminded herself that at least she had another option. "All right, thanks. I hope he feels better soon."

Vicky took the number for Benny and hung up. Then she called Benny. He answered on the first ring.

"Can I help you?" Benny sounded very enthusiastic.

"I was hoping that you could come out right away. We have an emergency at the Heavenly Highland Inn." Normally Vicky would never hire someone who she hadn't first met or researched, but there wasn't time to be picky. The longer the water was off, the more chance there was of angry guests, not to mention, with no water the kitchen was practically unusable.

"Sure, I can come out. What's the problem?"

"Somehow the sprinkler head in the banquet hall was broken and it began spraying water. We have the water off now, but the banquet hall is soaked. We need it fixed fast because our guests are without water." Her tone was urgent as she looked at the dripping tablecloths.

"Oh well, we can't have that. I'll be there in fifteen minutes." Benny sounded confident enough that Vicky felt reassured.

"Thank you, so much!" She willed herself not to think about what the repair bill would be.

Vicky hung up the phone and began gathering the rest of the tablecloths. As she did she noticed that one of them had a dark smudge on it. She stared at it for a long moment. The tablecloths were off-white in color and laundered every day. A stained tablecloth would never be put out on a table. It was impossible to tell what had caused the stain because the water had distorted its original shape. Vicky shook her head and added it to the rest of the pile.

"Ms. Vicky?" A timid voice drifted from the entrance of the hall. Vicky turned to see the new bellboy waiting for her.

"Blake, come in. Watch your step, the carpet is very wet. And please, just call me Vicky."

Blake nodded and stepped in carefully. Vicky had liked him immediately when she interviewed him. She had interviewed him because they needed someone urgently and Sarah had the day off because her little boy, Ethan, had a Parents' Day at school. Blake was only working at the inn a couple of days a week, because he was studying horticulture. He was very shy, but extremely polite and seemed quite mature.

"I need you to go down to the storage unit in the basement and bring up as many fans as you can find, please. We've had a bit of a problem here and we need to get the banquet hall in shape in time for dinner tonight. Okay?" She smiled at him.

"Basement, fans, fast." Blake nodded with each word he spoke. "You've got it."

"As quick as you can. You can ask some other staff for help if you need it. If you see Monica, send her in with a laundry cart, please." Vicky bundled up all of the wet tablecloths.

"Right away!" Blake ducked back out of the banquet hall. A minute later Monica arrived pushing a laundry cart. She rolled it right up to Vicky. Vicky tossed the tablecloths into the cart.

"Thanks, Monica. Listen, when you wash them one has some kind of stain. If it doesn't come clean we'll need to replace it. Okay?" She met Monica's eyes to be sure that she understood. Monica had been with them for some time, but Vicky had noticed lately that she seemed sleepy and distracted. Vicky assumed there might be some personal issues going on at home.

"Yes, I'll watch for it. Any idea how this happened?" Monica glanced up at the broken sprinkler.

Vicky frowned guiltily. She didn't want to mention the fact that she was fairly certain that it was her fault.

"I hope the plumber can tell us exactly how it happened." She looked up at the sprinkler. "I don't think it could have happened without something knocking into it."

"Do you think someone on the staff did it?" Monica spoke in a dramatic whisper. Vicky pursed her lips briefly. She didn't like gossip, especially when it involved the inn's employees, but she understood that Monica was just trying to get some idea of what had happened.

"No, I really don't think so." She swallowed back what she was really suspecting. She knew that she would have to admit the truth to Sarah, but she didn't want the entire staff knowing that she had done something so foolish. Recently, Vicky had hosted an indoor wedding reception in the banquet hall. She had gone a bit overboard with the decorations. She thought it was very likely that she had hit the sprinkler head with something as she hung it or carried it past. She hoped it wasn't the case, but she couldn't really think of any other explanation.

Chapter Three

As Vicky waited for the plumber to arrive, she tried not to focus on her mistake. Instead she did her best to fix it. She pushed the dining tables up against one wall so that the carpet would have a better chance of drying. She opened the door that led to the patio and opened all of the windows. It wasn't the warmest day, but she hoped that it would help, at least a little. Blake brought in several fans on a cart. He began lining them up and plugging them in. Vicky soon realized there weren't enough sockets for all of the fans they would need.

"See if we have any extension cords that we can use. We're going to need a lot of air power." Vicky sighed. She turned towards the banquet hall doors to help Blake and nearly barreled into a large man. He looked like a bear, not only because of his size, but because of the thick, woolly curls on the top of his head, his long beard and thick, hairy arms. Vicky moved back just before she would have collided with him. "Excuse me, Sir, I didn't see you there."

"It's quite all right. I'm Benny, the plumber." He raised a thick eyebrow. "I'm assuming this is where the problem is."

"Yes. I sure hope you can fix it, and fast. I'm afraid that the sprinkler might have gotten hit and knocked out of place." She pointed out the damaged sprinkler.

"That doesn't look great." Benny squinted at it. "Lucky for you I have parts in my van. I'm going to get this fixed up for you no problem."

"Great!" Vicky sighed with relief. "Thanks for coming out so quickly."

"Oh, trust me, I'm just glad to have some work. Things have been very slow lately." He offered her a broad smile. Vicky smiled politely in return. She wasn't sure if she had made the right decision. In her experience plumbers were always in demand. Was Benny such a bad plumber that he didn't get a lot of work? She hadn't even checked on his license. It was too late to turn back now, and he had said that he could fix the problem. She gritted her teeth and told herself to stick with it and see how it turned out.

Vicky watched as Benny lumbered over to the sprinkler. He grabbed one of the chairs that was upholstered in the same off-white material as the tablecloths. Vicky was too horrified to protest as he climbed up onto the chair with his grimy shoes. By the time she found her voice it was too late. Benny was already perched on top of it. The damage was done. He reached up and began tugging at the sprinkler.

"How did you say this happened?" He looked down at her with a puzzled expression.

"I guess maybe I banged it with a decoration when I was setting up for a wedding." Vicky frowned. She felt terribly guilty for causing the trouble.

"You?" Benny looked down at Vicky with disbelief. "You and what army?"

"Excuse me?" Vicky frowned. Her willingness to see the humor in the situation was quickly fading.

"I'm sorry, but unless you were decorating with a sledge hammer there is no way that you could have done this. It's practically snapped off." He shook his head. "No, I'd have to say that someone did this on purpose."

"You're sure?" Vicky asked as she looked up at him. "I don't know why anyone would do such a thing." She was genuinely confused. It hadn't occurred to her that someone might have done it on purpose. Perhaps by accident, as she had suspected she had, but to willingly destroy one of the sprinkler heads? Why would anyone want to do that?

"Oh, I've seen it before." Benny chuckled. "Probably some little upstart bed and breakfast that is trying to empty out the competition."

"What do you mean?" Vicky stepped closer to him. She peered up at the damaged sprinkler.

"I mean, if your guests are forced to flee a flood, then they will find the nearest place to finish out their vacation. I wouldn't be surprised if that was the reason for this damage. But don't worry, I can get this piece off and replace it. I'll only need about an hour." He tilted his head towards the fans she had lined up. "But I can tell you, it's going to take a lot longer to dry out the carpet with those tiny things. I've got a couple of industrial fans in my van. I'll bring them in when I finish."

"Thanks." Vicky smiled, but she was troubled. She wondered if Benny could be right. Did someone who owned another inn damage the sprinkler on purpose? If so how did they even get in to do it? She hadn't heard of any new inns opening in the area, but then because of the popularity of the Heavenly Highland Inn, there hadn't been much need to keep an eye on the competition.

As Benny stepped down from the chair to get the part, Vicky stared at the footprints that he left behind. Vicky suddenly knew what had caused the stain on the tablecloth. It had probably been a footprint! She assumed that someone had climbed up on the table to damage the sprinkler. She shuddered at the thought of someone so bent on destruction being in the inn without her knowing it. Was it a staff member? Was it a guest? Was it someone who had slipped in from outside? Her mind spun with the possibilities.

As the plumber worked on the sprinkler, Vicky did her best to position the fans to dry the carpet as fast as possible. It was hard to focus on fixing the problem, when she was worried about what might happen next. If someone had been determined enough to damage property, would they give up after one attempt?

Chapter Four

Ida stopped in her room to check her makeup and hair before she headed off to Roman's room. She was looking forward to moving into Vicky's apartment so that she would have a bigger closet. The closet in the guest room she lived in was bursting at the seams. Once she was sure she looked gorgeous enough to meet Roman, she headed down the hall to his room. She noticed a few staff members running back and forth as they attempted to help with the situation in the banquet hall. The eager, young bellboy almost ran right into Ida.

"Excuse me, I'm so sorry!" He blushed.

"It's quite all right. You're in a rush. Where are you off to?"

"Oh, I'm collecting fans for the banquet hall." He looked past her anxiously.

"The fans are in the basement." Ida narrowed her eyes. "What are you doing on the third floor?"

"I got those." Blake began to walk past her. "I was just checking the storage rooms to see if there were any more."

"Oh." Ida nodded. "Okay, I hope you find some."

"Thanks." Blake hurried past her.

As Ida neared Roman's door, she saw Monica wheeling a laundry cart. She waved hello to her, but Monica just stared straight past her. She was moving slowly. Ida noticed because it was a big change from how fast Blake had been moving. Ida assumed the young woman must have something weighing on her mind. Then she saw it. Roman's room. She was surprised that he didn't have security at the door, but she knew that he liked to appear as if he was no different to the rest of the population. If he had a security detail he probably kept them at a distance.

Ida took a deep breath and reminded herself to relax. Then she walked up to the door. She could barely contain her excitement. Carefully, she fluffed her hair to make sure that it was in order. Then she knocked lightly on the door. After a few moments the door opened. Ida stared into the gleaming eyes that she had seen on posters and on television. His slicked back, silver hair made Ida's heart flutter. His lips parted to reveal a voice as smooth as silk.

"I'm sorry, I wasn't expecting anyone." He frowned as he looked at Ida. "Did we have an appointment?"

"No, no appointment." Ida felt flustered now that she was actually face to face with the man she admired so much. "My nieces own the inn and they asked me to offer you a tour of the town, or perhaps just the grounds if you prefer. Your campaign manager can come along as well..."

"Wow, what a wonderful idea." He smiled at her. "Are you sure you have enough time to spend it with me?"

"I'm sure," Ida said quickly. "I was wondering if you might like to start with a snack at a little café I know very well."

"That sounds marvelous! Trevor is in the room across the hall. Let's see if he wants to join us." He walked across the hall and knocked twice. No one answered so Roman knocked again. Ida stood behind him. "That's weird I thought he said he was going to stay in his room to do some work. Maybe he changed his mind." As he started to turn a slender man who was about six feet tall with light brown hair walked down the hall towards them.

"There you are," Roman said.

"Were you looking for me?" Trevor asked. "I just decided to duck out and look at the flowers for a bit. Such beauty."

"Trevor has a thing for all things natural." He turned to Ida. "This is Trevor my campaign manager. Trev, this is Ida." Roman gestured to Ida. Trevor nodded to Ida in acknowledgment. "Ida runs the inn with her nieces, She is going to take me on a tour of the premises and the town. Would you like to join us?"

"No, thank you." He shook his head. "I was hoping to go through some plans with you."

"Maybe later, Trevor."

"We have to go through it sometime." Trevor's eyes grew cold.

"And we will," Roman said. "Why don't you do some of your scientific reading."

"No, no plant study today." Trevor smiled slightly. "I need to finish putting together some campaign presentations."

"We can discuss them later," Roman said. "Maybe after we have dinner?"

"We were going to work over dinner, remember?"

"You need to relax, Trevor. Work can wait till later."

"I would prefer to have an early night, tonight," Trevor said as he moved a small cardboard box he was holding to his left hand and unlocked the door to his room.

"Okay, I'll see you at dinner. Don't work too hard."

"Have fun," Trevor said dryly before he closed the door.

"Sorry about that, he loves his work a bit too much." Roman laughed slightly as he turned towards his room. "Give me a moment and I'll meet you downstairs. All right?"

"Great!" Ida couldn't hide her grin. As she made her way back down to the lobby Ida thought about her boyfriend, Rex. He was away on a long motorcycle ride and she missed him. She was glad that she had the opportunity to show Roman around while Rex was out of town. She was surprised when she had told Rex that Roman was staying there and that she was going to offer to give him a tour that he was just as excited as she was. Apparently, Rex was a fan and like Ida hoped Roman became governor. She herself had a little crush on Roman and even though she would never do anything, as she loved Rex, she still felt a little guilty. She was a little troubled as she reached the lobby. She noticed Sarah was at the front desk with a woman.

"Freida, I can assure you that we will do our very best to accommodate anything that you need."

"Oh good, hon, I don't like to make a fuss, there's just a few things that I like a certain way." The petite, red-haired woman smiled at Sarah. Ida walked towards the front desk at the same moment that Vicky was walking in from the banquet hall.

"Aunt Ida, it didn't go well?" Vicky asked.

"Huh?" Ida nearly jumped at the sound of Vicky's voice just behind her. "Oh, it went fine actually. I'm taking him into town for a little snack."

"That's great." Vicky smiled. "I'm glad that you're getting to enjoy yourself."

"What's that supposed to mean?" Ida asked in a defensive tone. "I won't be enjoying myself, no enjoying will be going on, this is strictly inn business."

Vicky raised an eyebrow at her aunt's sudden tirade. Normally she would question it, but she had so much on her mind that she decided to let it slide. It had been a rough morning and she didn't blame her aunt for being on edge.

"Okay, Aunt Ida, just let me know if you need anything." Vicky stepped past her towards the front desk. She smiled warmly at the guest who was checking in.

"Vicky, I'm glad you're here." Sarah looked at her sister with a hint of relief. "This is Freida Frans, she's staying in 310. We need to make sure that she has a few things in her room."

"Of course, I'll get Monica right on it." Vicky started to turn away. Then suddenly it struck her that the woman's name was very familiar. She turned back as she recalled just who she was. Freida was well known for writing the most scathing gossip articles. She always seemed to have the scoop on every celebrity and socialite, whether it turned out to be true or not rarely mattered as people loved to read all about the dirt she dug up. Before Vicky could say a word about who she was, Roman Blade stepped out of the elevator and walked towards the front desk. As Roman stepped up beside the front desk, his eyes narrowed. He looked directly at Freida.

"Well, isn't it convenient that you've chosen to stay here?" He cleared his throat and set his jaw.

Freida peered in his direction. She scrunched up her nose with disgust. "Had I known that you were staying here, Roman, I would have kept on driving right past."

Sarah and Vicky exchanged a look of concern as the sparks flew between the two guests.

"Are you really going to tell me that you had no idea I was staying here, Freida? You've told some whoppers in your time, but this one takes the cake." He shook his head dismissively.

"Whoppers?" Freida huffed. "Just because you don't like the truth doesn't make it any less valid. I think that your arrogance is showing again, Roman."

"My arrogance? You are practically stalking me, Freida!" Roman exclaimed. "It's sad really."

"I am staying at an inn, not lurking outside your house. Maybe, if you weren't so self-important, Roman, you would see the real needs of the people." With that Freida pushed past Roman and began heading for the stairs. Sarah chased after her to show her to her room. Roman watched her go with a seething grimace. Then he turned to look at Vicky and Ida.

"I apologize, Ladies, please don't think less of me for my display. That woman is the bane of my existence." He sighed.

"No need to apologize, Roman, you're entitled to your opinion." Ida offered him her arm. "Maybe I can take your mind off such troubling thoughts."

"I would greatly appreciate it." Roman smiled.

Vicky studied him as he curved his arm around Ida's. She was a little taken back by the way he had spoken to Freida. Most politicians were careful about saving face as much as possible. She was sure that he and Freida must have a long history. She nearly got caught up in it, but turned her focus back to the plumber. She had come out to give Sarah an update that the sprinkler had been fixed, but that they had bigger problems. With Sarah gone, and Roman and Ida headed out the front door, Vicky was left to think about just how they were going to handle lunch.

Chapter Five

Ida strolled with Roman down the narrow path towards the town square. Roman seemed to be quite pleased by the scenery.

"To be honest, I haven't seen so much green in a very long time." His voice was wistful as he watched a butterfly drift by.

"It is beautiful here. Just enough country while still being close to quaint little shops and not too far from the city." Ida smiled. She was enjoying spending her time with Roman and promoting the inn to him. She thought about Rex and how different Roman was from Rex who was burly with plenty of hair. Roman was neat and tidy. She could appreciate that in a man even though she loved Rex's rugged looks.

All of a sudden Ida felt as if someone was following them. She turned around to see a young man in a black suit.

"That's my security." Roman smiled. "Seeing as I'm taking a break from campaigning I only have one guy with me when I leave the premises. At least I don't have a permanent shadow at the moment."

As they continued towards the town, Ida noticed that Roman walked with a slight limp in his gait. She didn't think it would be polite to mention it. However, when they neared the bottom of the path he stumbled slightly. Ida reached out to steady him.

"Are you all right?" she asked as she met his eyes with concern.

"I'm sorry." He sighed. "I have a bit of a trick knee. An old war injury." He flashed her a smile. Ida raised an eyebrow, but she didn't question further. She knew that many politicians had been in the military. He straightened up and began to walk comfortably again. Ida took the time to show him the ice cream shop, the antique boutique, and even the small museum that featured the history of the area. Vicky had been right, it wasn't that historical, but there was always something that drew the tourists in.

As they waited for an order of french fries at the local deli, Ida took a close look at Roman. She noticed that his gaze was constantly shifting. He didn't just gaze at the counter, or the pictures on the wall. He was constantly sweeping the deli. If he noticed a person, he would flash a charming smile and offer a friendly nod. Ida wasn't surprised by that, as he was in the middle of a campaign, but the constant flicking of his eyes was a little unsettling. She wondered if it might be leftover trauma from his time in the Army.

"Roman, are you okay?" Ida asked. "You seem restless."

"Oh Ida, do forgive me if I've been neglectful." He sighed. "Ever since I laid eyes on Freida, my nerves have been on edge. She's likely following us right now. She's always looking for something to use against me."

"That must be a terrible thing to have someone following you around like that," Ida said sympathetically. "You'd think that she could find better ways to spend her time."

"Oh, I'm sure she will soon move on to someone else. She can try to dig for as much dirt on me as she wants, she won't find anything to sink her teeth into." He offered a pleasant smile. Ida smiled back at him. She couldn't help but be drawn to his personable nature. She was being reassured in her belief that he would make a fantastic governor.

"Ah, here are the fries." He reached for his wallet.

"No, I insist." Ida slid the owner of the deli payment for the snack as well as an ample tip. She always spoiled the local businesses and she usually got special treatment in return for it. "Trust me, once you taste these, you're never going to want to leave."

"I believe it." He chuckled. Ida noticed that Roman's security guard was standing by the entrance to the deli. They walked over to an empty table and settled in to dine on the french fries. Ida waited for his reaction. She smiled when his eyes widened. "Wow, these have a real kick!"

"Jalapeno cheese." Ida smiled devilishly. She laughed slightly as she remembered the first time she had shared a plate of the fries with Rex. He had gone running for the bathroom as there had not been any water on the table. Roman however handled the spice just fine and continued to chow down on the fries.

"I don't think I've ever tasted a better fry."

Ida was pleased that she was showing him a good time. She wondered how things were going back at the inn.

***

Vicky walked out onto the patio. There was furniture there for outside dining, but she had to add extra tables and chairs to accommodate everyone. She needed to arrange it carefully to give the guests a little more privacy and freedom to eat alone if they desired. As she began shuffling the patio furniture around she heard a voice drift down from above her.

"Yes, he's here. I knew he would be." Freida laughed a little. "You should have seen his face when he saw me. I thought he was going to lose it." She sounded very amused. "He must be worried that I'll ruin his campaign. You know his sidekick will do anything to win."

Vicky glanced up to see that she was standing on the balcony of her third floor room. She frowned at the pleasure she was taking in making Roman squirm. Before passing judgment she told herself to keep her thoughts to herself. She had no idea what the tension between Freida and Roman was about. She imagined that Freida had drummed up some rumor against Roman, but Vicky didn't read Freida's articles, so she couldn't be sure. She focused on moving the furniture and spacing it apart. As she did, the conversation above her continued.

"I know, I just think it's delightful that he thinks he deserves some kind of special treatment. That's the last thing we need in a government official, one more regular guy thinking he's some kind of superstar because he buys enough votes. I'm not normally political, but this guy, I just can't let him get away with his con artist ways."

Vicky was intrigued by what Freida was saying. It didn't sound as if she was discussing rumors at all. It sounded like Freida might have some solid proof or at least a good reason to have a problem with Roman. Vicky made a mental note to ask the maids and bellboys to ensure that Freida and Roman were kept apart. The last thing she wanted was some kind of argument or fight to have to deal with. The flooded banquet hall was stressful enough. As she moved the last chair into place, she heard Freida again. It was hard not to, as the woman spoke as if she was shouting through the phone to wherever the person on the other end of the line was.

"Don't worry, I'm not afraid of him. He can threaten me as much as he wants, but he's not as powerful as he thinks."

After those words everything grew quiet. Vicky tried not to focus on the implications of the statement. Was Roman dangerous? Had he threatened Freida? She gritted her teeth and took a step back from the arranged furniture. She had created a lovely little oasis complete with umbrellas angled away from one another so that they created an intimate shield. She added a touch of music and some additional foliage. The feeling was rather tropical because it was beside the pool. She was sure that most of the guests would be pleased with having the option to dine outside. She headed from the patio to the kitchen to tell Henry about the lunch options. As she pushed through the kitchen door she noticed a figure hovering near the pantry. Henry usually didn't allow anyone in his pantry, so she assumed that it was him.

"Chef Henry, do you have a minute?" Vicky called out. The figure turned slowly to face her. She saw that it was the young bellboy, Blake. He was blushing furiously. "Blake, what are you doing? You shouldn't be anywhere near the pantry."

"I know, I'm sorry." He frowned. "I thought maybe there might be some scraps of food inside that weren't being used."

"Scraps of food?" Vicky narrowed her eyes. "Blake, if you're hungry just ask Chef Henry I'm sure he has extra food stowed away somewhere."

"I was going to, but he was so upset about the banquet hall, and he's a little..." Blake cleared his throat. "I'm a little afraid of him."

"Of Chef Henry?" Vicky laughed. "Trust me, he's not the least bit scary."

"I'm sorry," Blake repeated his apology. It looked to Vicky like he was sweating. She felt a pang of sympathy for him. She remembered what it was like to be so shy.

"Just check next time with Chef Henry first, okay?" She raised an eyebrow. "There are some apples over there if you want to grab one." She pointed out the basket of apples on the butcher's block in the center of the kitchen.

"Thank you." Blake nodded. He snatched up one of the apples and hurried out of the kitchen. Just as he was leaving, Henry walked into the kitchen.

"Vicky, how can I help?" he asked.

"I just wanted to let you know that I have set up the patio for lunch service. I think it will be fine, and hopefully we'll be able to seat everyone inside for dinner." She looked hopeful as she glanced out the window that overlooked the courtyard. "There's a chance of rain tonight and it might be too cold for anyone to eat outside."

"I'm sure it will be fine." Henry nodded. "Let me know if you need help with anything. Has the plumber turned the water back on?"

"Yes. He fixed the sprinkler and everything should be back to normal now." Vicky kept the information about the sprinkler being damaged on purpose to herself. As she left the kitchen she caught Sarah in the hallway.

"Sarah! I need to talk to you." Vicky hurried over to her. Sarah looked drained as she leaned up against the hallway wall.

"What is it?" She frowned.

"Did you get everything settled with Freida?" Vicky asked.

"As best I could," Sarah said. "I'm not sure if that woman is ever satisfied."

Vicky decided not to mention the conversation she had overheard. Sarah didn't need any more stress than what would be caused by what Vicky was about to tell her.

"The sprinkler is fixed, and the water is back on, but the plumber made it clear to me that the sprinkler had to have been intentionally damaged." Vicky narrowed her eyes. "Someone worked very hard to make sure that the sprinkler was broken."

"What?" Sarah threw her hands up into the air. "This is ridiculous. Who would do something like that? Now, we're going to lose guests, I just know it, and Vicky you know with the rest of the renovations we're planning we can't afford to lose any money. We've got two big names staying at our inn and no restaurant or banquet hall to serve dinner in, and..."

Vicky hugged her sister warmly. "Just take a breath, Sarah. It's going to be okay."

Sarah took a deep breath and hugged her sister back. "Thanks, Vicky, I needed that. I know I'm flipping out."

"You have reason to, but it's going to be okay." Vicky gave her sister an encouraging smile. "I have the fans on full blast in the banquet hall with all of the windows open. I'm sure that once the carpets have a few hours to dry out, it will be fine for dinner tonight."

"You're right." Sarah nodded. "I'm just a little extra tense after that exchange between Freida and Roman. We'll have to make sure to keep them apart."

Vicky almost told her about what she had heard Freida saying, but she didn't want to upset Sarah more.

"Why don't you go take a break for a bit? There's nothing to do right now. I can keep an eye on the guests." Vicky glanced into the lobby. Everything was quiet.

"Okay, that's a good idea. I'll take a walk around the property." As Sarah turned and walked away Vicky felt relieved that she was able to do something to ease Sarah's mind. Her sister, though not much older than her, had always been more mature. She took responsibility for everything that needed to be done, or that went wrong. As a mother of two young boys she had her hands full at home too.

Chapter Six

A half hour before dinner, Vicky went to check on the banquet hall. Before she could reach it, she was nearly run over by Monica. The woman who had been moving so slow early in the day was racing down the hallway. Vicky jumped out of the way just in time to avoid a collision. She narrowly missed backing into Trevor. When she turned around to apologize, he was already in the elevator so she continued towards Monica.

"Monica!" Vicky exclaimed. "What are you doing?"

"I'm so sorry, Vicky." Monica stopped and turned to face Vicky. "I was trying to get to the front door before Freida Frans could."

"Why?" Vicky stared at her in disbelief.

"Because she's got her camera, and she was going to take pictures of Ida and Roman Blade." She lowered her eyes shamefully. Vicky got the sense that there was a lot more to the story than she was sharing.

"How does she even know that Aunt Ida is showing Roman around town?" Vicky asked, though she already had her suspicions.

"You see, I was placing some fresh flowers in Freida's room, as she requested. When I did, Freida started asking me a few questions about Roman's room." Monica grimaced. "I didn't think it was a big deal since the rooms are practically identical. Then she asked me if he was there now." She stopped talking.

"Monica?" Vicky frowned. "Did you answer her?"

"I did. I don't know why, I guess I had just fallen into conversation with her, and I didn't think about Roman's privacy. I just told her that he had been out all day with Ida." She shook her head. "I know I shouldn't have, but the words had already come out of my mouth. I'm sorry, Vicky. As soon as she heard that she grabbed her camera and said she was going to catch the two 'love birds' and splash it all over the newspapers."

Vicky's eyes widened. She knew that Ida was only enjoying Roman's company, but Freida could make a scandal out of anything. If she took those pictures of Roman and Ida together, not only would Roman's reputation be in question, but Rex would likely see the photographs as well and might be upset by them. She heard the ding of the elevator announcing that it had reached the lobby.

"We are going to have a serious conversation about guest privacy, Monica," Vicky said. Before Monica could defend herself Vicky hurried away to confront Freida at the elevator.

Freida stepped out of the elevator. She had her camera slung over her shoulder and a determined smirk on her lips. Vicky knew that she had to intervene fast if she was going to prevent her from creating a scandal that would not only involve Ida, but also the Heavenly Highland Inn.

"Freida! I'm glad I caught you." Vicky smiled warmly.

"I'm sorry, I'm on my way out." Freida tried to brush past Vicky.

"Wait just a minute, please." Vicky lightly touched the woman's arm. She knew that Freida had the power to write a scathing article about the inn and cause quite a bit of damage to their reputation. She had to handle this very carefully.

"I'm sorry, I'm in a bit of a rush." Freida looked at her crossly.

"I just wanted to be sure that you had everything that you needed. Did you find fresh towels in your bathroom?" Vicky moved between Freida and the door.

"I did. They're fine. Everything's fine. Now, I must be going." Freida tried to step around Vicky. Vicky moved swiftly to block her way.

"Oh, I'm so glad. I have to admit, I'm a little star struck. I'm one of your biggest fans, and to have you staying here is a true honor." Vicky forced her smile to grow even wider.

"I think it's great that you're a fan, but right now, I'm trying to work." Freida met Vicky's eyes with a look of warning. "Kindly move out of my way."

"I'm so sorry. I didn't mean to prevent you from working. Maybe I could tag along?" Vicky widened her eyes to show how eager she was. "It would be amazing to see you in action."

Freida gazed at her skeptically. She looked as if she was about to call Vicky out on her terrible acting. Instead her scowl faded and a hint of arrogance entered her expression.

"Not too many people have the opportunity to see me in action." She tilted her head to the side. "I guess it wouldn't hurt to have you along. You might be able to help me navigate the area."

"Oh great!" Vicky nodded. "I'm looking forward to the opportunity."

"Great, well I'm headed out now." She began to walk towards the door. Vicky suddenly realized the mistake that she had made. She needed to check on the banquet hall to be sure it was ready for dinner service, but instead she had committed herself to wandering the area with Freida. Luckily, before she had to comply with Freida's wishes, Ida swung the front door of the lobby open. Roman held it open as she stepped inside. Then Roman stepped in behind her. He slid his arm through Ida's. Freida raised her camera, ready to pounce. Vicky jumped in front of the camera before Freida could snap the picture.

"Are we leaving now?" Vicky asked. Freida kept trying to get around Vicky to take the picture. Vicky kept moving in the same direction to block Roman and Ida. Ida caught sight of the two and hurried Roman to the elevator. Freida groaned with exasperation as the elevator doors slid shut.

"I should have known." She shook her head. "All you're trying to do is stop me from doing my job. You're no fan of mine."

Vicky pursed her lips. She knew that she had gotten herself and the inn into a bit of a problem. She didn't want to have Freida as an enemy.

"I'm sorry, why do you think that?"

"Why do I think that?" Freida nearly shouted. "You blocked my camera!"

"Did I get in the way? Were you trying to get pictures of my Aunt Ida?" Vicky did her best to appear innocent. "Why in the world would you want pictures of her?"

"Because she was on a date with Roman Blade," Freida spat out angrily.

"Oh, she most certainly wasn't. I'm glad I was able to stop you from making that mistake. You would have been terribly embarrassed when the truth came out. You see, my sister and I asked our aunt if she could introduce Roman to the area, in the hopes of making him aware of what our town might need if he were to become governor. She was simply doing what we requested, nothing romantic about it." Vicky laughed. "I'm glad I was able to make that clear."

Freida glared at her. Vicky sensed that Freida could see right through her act, but if she could, she didn't say so. She simply turned on her heel and walked away. Vicky felt the tension leave her body as Freida disappeared in the elevator. She wasn't sure whether Freida would try to damage the reputation of the hotel with a hateful article, but at least she wouldn't have ammunition that would hurt Roman's campaign and could impact Ida's relationship with Rex.

Just as Vicky was about to go to the banquet hall she noticed a basket of fruit on the front counter. She walked over and looked at the delivery slip. It said 'Heavenly Highland Inn-Room 301'. There was a card attached that had no writing on the envelope. She immediately presumed that a delivery man had just left it there when the counter was unattended and she wasn't sure how long it had been there. She picked it up just as Monica walked through the lobby.

"Monica," Vicky said as she pulled off the delivery slip and put it in the trashcan. Monica looked timidly towards Vicky, as if she was waiting for Vicky to get angry with her.

"Yes, Vicky," she said with downcast eyes.

"Are you okay to deliver this to the third floor for me, please?" Vicky asked. "I have to check on the banquet hall."

"Right away," Monica said with relief as she grabbed the basket of fruit.

"It's for room 301. Thank you." Vicky smiled as Monica walked off. As Vicky turned back towards the banquet hall, she realized she had no idea if it would be okay and it was dangerously close to dinner time.

Chapter Seven

As Vicky started walking towards the banquet hall she hoped it would be fine as she had promised Sarah it would be. As if the thought of her had summoned her, Sarah walked through the front door of the lobby.

"Did I just see Aunt Ida?" Sarah asked. "I was going to find out how the tour went with Roman."

"They're upstairs." Vicky pointed to the elevator.

"How is the banquet hall?" Sarah asked.

"I honestly haven't checked yet." Vicky grimaced. "I got distracted." Again she decided not to reveal the whole truth to Sarah. She didn't want her sister to be worried that Freida was upset with Vicky or the inn.

"That's all right, let's take a look together." Sarah's face grew tense as she walked towards the banquet hall. Vicky kept an even pace beside her. She kept telling herself that everything would be fine. The carpet would be dry, or at least dry enough that people wouldn't notice it.

Through the glass panes in the double doors that led into the banquet hall the carpets looked great.

"You see, Sarah, there was never anything to worry about." Vicky smiled as she opened the doors to the banquet hall. The carpet was spotless, and the tables were ready to go. The room looked great. But there was another problem.

"Oh, what is that?" Sarah grimaced and covered her nose.

"I don't know." Vicky pinched her nose as well. The smell that wafted out of the banquet hall was so overpowering that it made Vicky's stomach churn. She noticed that the windows she had made sure were all open to help diffuse any lingering smell, were all closed.

"We certainly can't host dinner in there!" Sarah's voice grew higher as she became more agitated. "Now, what are we going to do?"

"Well, we still have the patio set up from lunch. It is chilly outside, but it's not too cold and it doesn't look like it's going to rain after all. The guests can either sit on the patio or have room service." Vicky frowned. "We're going to have to move fast to get room service set up. It looks like it's going to be a busy night."

Sarah looked dismayed, but she snapped into action. "All right, let Chef Henry know, and make sure that everyone is available to help."

"I'm sorry, Sarah, I should have checked on the banquet hall earlier. I know I left those windows open!" Vicky felt her heart pound with anger. She wondered who would have closed the windows. Then she realized that someone had to have set up the tables. Some well-meaning staff member had probably thought it was best to close the windows to keep the chilly air out.

"No time for that now, Vicky." Sarah did look a little annoyed as she turned to face her sister. "What we need to do is get on top of this before it gets out of hand."

"You're right."

Vicky ran off towards the kitchen. Chef Henry was already preparing some food for the evening meal.

"We have a problem." Vicky stood in the middle of the kitchen.

"No banquet hall?" Henry looked up at her. Vicky nodded.

"We've got outside ready and we are probably going to be doing a lot of room service." Vicky cringed.

"Okay, all right, let's get to it!" Chef Henry clapped his hands. He began lining up trays for room service. Sarah arranged for notices to be dropped off at each room announcing that the banquet hall would be closed for dinner service and that the patio was set up for dinner, but all guests were welcome to use their room service menu at no extra charge. Not long after that she joined the others in the kitchen. The phone hanging on the wall of the kitchen began ringing.

Although some guests were happy to sit outside in the cool weather, the orders for room service were coming in so fast that Henry could barely keep up. His staff were working as hard as they could, but they didn't have much experience with having to cook so quickly. Normally, the dinner service was spread out over a few hours, but because Sarah had just let the guests know they seemed to all want dinner at once. When a big pot hit the floor due to slippery hands, Vicky nearly jumped out of her skin. Everyone in the kitchen went silent for a moment.

"It's going to be okay, everyone is doing great." Vicky snatched the empty pot up from the floor and put it back on the stove. "The waiters are busy with serving the guests on the patio, but I'm going to get some of the other staff to help the bellboys with delivering room service."

After asking Monica to help with the food delivery and helping herself, they managed to get through food service without any drama. Although Vicky was worn-out, she decided to go check on the banquet hall before helping to tidy up for the day.

"Oh, Vicky, you look exhausted." Sarah frowned as she walked into the kitchen just as Vicky was exiting. "I can finish up here, go get some rest."

Vicky was tired. She didn't want to admit it, but she had worked harder in one night than she had in months. She nodded at Sarah.

"If you're sure," Vicky said.

"I am."

"I'm just going to check on the fans one more time and make sure that the night staff know not to close the windows."

"I'll do that, you go to bed." She smiled at Vicky. "You really came through tonight, Vicky. We managed to avoid a disaster."

Vicky offered a weak smile in return. Though she agreed that they had pleased the guests with room service and alfresco dining, she also knew that she had upset Freida. Freida might even be working on an article right at that moment. An article that could tear apart the inn's reputation. But there was nothing that Vicky could do about that, and it wouldn't help matters for Sarah to be worried about it as well.

"Good night, Sarah." Vicky gave her a quick hug and then headed to her apartment. As she walked through the lobby she saw Trevor and Roman heading towards the elevator.

"Why don't you come to my room and we can have a drink," Roman said.

"Not tonight, I'm tired."

"Oh come on, I'll have a drink and you can have a tea. And we can talk about that scientific stuff you love, flowers and vegetables."

"Not tonight."

"Okay you win, we can even work if you really want." Roman laughed slightly. "You've never been one to turn down work."

"In the morning," Trevor said.

"Wow, you must be tired." Vicky watched them as they stepped into the elevator. "The morning it is." The doors slid shut.

It sounded like Roman wanted some company. She imagined that it could get quite lonely on the campaign trail.

Vicky continued walking towards her apartment. It was not a long walk from the lobby to her apartment door. She knew it would be a bit longer when the new house was built. It also meant she would have a little more privacy.

Vicky opened the door to her apartment with the turn of her sore wrist. She could barely lift her arms. After all of the lifting and moving, she was exhausted. She stepped inside to the smell of dinner cooking. The aroma brought a smile to her lips. Her mind drifted dreamily to her amazing husband. She hadn't expected him to be home as he usually worked later into the evening. It was a special treat to be greeted by him and a hot meal.

"Hey, sweetheart." Mitchell stepped out of the small kitchen. "How are you doing?"

"Great, now that I'm home." Vicky hugged him warmly, though it made her arms ache to do so. "One flooded banquet hall, and a full on dinner service, I'm still breathing."

"I'm sorry you had such a rough day. Dinner still has about twenty minutes to go. Can I interest you in a massage?" His gaze was warm as he settled it on her.

"Oh yes, absolutely you can." Vicky smiled at him. "How did I get this lucky?"

"Just remember that when I have to live and breathe a case for a week or two." Mitchell tugged her down onto the couch beside him.

"I will, I promise." She sighed as he began massaging her shoulders.

"So, how did the hall get flooded?" He continued to work his way down along her shoulder blades. Vicky felt as if she was drifting right into paradise.

"Someone broke one of the sprinklers. The plumber said that it looked like it was done on purpose," Vicky said. "I have no idea who would have done something like that."

"I don't like the sound of that. Maybe I should take a look tomorrow?" Mitchell ran his hands back up to the top of her shoulders and then began to massage her upper arms. Vicky felt herself melt as the pain in her arms faded under his touch.

"I'm not too worried. I'm more concerned about the politician and the gossip columnist staying at the inn." She leaned back against his chest and he wrapped his arms around her waist.

"That is bad, but wait until you hear what happened to me today." He grinned as he kissed the top of her head.

"It couldn't possibly have been worse," she murmured and closed her eyes.

"I think maybe it was." He laughed. "We got a call about a dead body."

"What? Why is that funny?" Vicky was genuinely confused. She opened her eyes and looked up at him with shock.

"Just wait, you'll understand soon. Now relax." Vicky closed her eyes again. "So we responded to this call. We didn't know what to expect, as it was in the woods. We thought perhaps a jogger had a medical event, or worst case scenario foul play. When we got there, there wasn't a body that we could find. We got the hiker who called it in to show us where he had seen the body. He pointed out what looked like tiny fingers sticking out of the leaves. So, of course we were horrified. I brushed the leaves back, and instead of a dead body, I found a possum."

"A possum?" Vicky laughed. "That had to be pretty surprising."

"Not as surprising as discovering that he wasn't dead at all! When I moved the leaves the thing sprang into action and ran right across my shoes. I have to admit I screamed." He lowered his voice and hung his head slightly. "It was a very high-pitched scream."

"Oh Mitchell, that is pretty bad." Vicky couldn't help but chuckle at what he had described.

"So, I'd say we both had rough days." Mitchell helped her to her feet. "Let's forget about them, and lose ourselves in a delicious meal. Sound good?"

"Oh yes, very." Vicky followed him into the kitchen. As she helped him get the food onto plates, she did try to push the events of the day out of her mind. It was hard not to bring work home with her when she lived inside the inn. Maybe when their house was built she would be able to close the door, and truly have a life away from the inn.

Chapter Eight

Early the next morning Vicky woke up to the sound of Mitchell closing and locking the door. She realized he must have had an early call. She pulled herself out of bed. She wanted to get to the banquet hall and inspect it. Her mind was still troubled by who might have caused the damage to the sprinkler. She also wanted to be sure that the banquet hall was ready for breakfast service. She dressed quickly and headed out into the lobby. Trevor was coming out of the lift.

"Good morning, Trevor," Vicky said. "How are you this morning?"

"Good, thank you," Trevor said as he continued towards the door. "I'm just going to look at the beautiful flowers you have in your gardens here, enjoy the morning sun and do a little reading," he said as he tapped a large book in his hand. Vicky looked at it, but she couldn't see the front. It looked like a textbook.

"Sounds wonderful," Vicky said. "Enjoy."

When she reached the front desk Sarah was already there with two cups of coffee.

"Great minds think alike." Sarah smiled as she handed Vicky a coffee. "I already checked on the banquet hall. It's just fine. I think that breakfast service will go smoothly. I also sent Monica upstairs to collect the dinner trays."

"Did she look okay to you?" Vicky asked. "I might have been a little harsh on her yesterday." She took a sip from her mug of coffee.

"Harsh, why?" Sarah blinked. Vicky suddenly remembered that she hadn't told Sarah anything about the encounter between her and Freida, or the fact that it was Monica who had innocently spilled the information to Freida. It was too early in the morning for her to keep up with everything.

"Oh uh, no reason really. She was just moving rather slow." Vicky frowned.

"That's because her baby's teething." Sarah smiled a little. "I remember those days. I'm sure she's not getting much sleep, she looked like she was struggling to stay awake today. Take it easy on her, okay?"

"Okay..." Vicky stopped talking as a piercing scream carried through the inn. Vicky nearly dropped her coffee mug as her entire body jolted at the sound. Sarah's eyes flew wide open with alarm. It was not the type of scream that could be explained away. It was the type of scream that made hot blood run cold.

Vicky and Sarah rushed up the stairs to the third floor. Neither wanted to take the time to wait for the elevator. Vicky raced ahead of Sarah and headed in the direction of the scream. When she found the right room Vicky barreled through the door and nearly tripped over Monica who was frozen where she stood.

"Freida." Monica pointed a trembling finger towards the dinette table that was set up near the balcony. Vicky saw Freida who appeared to have fallen asleep with her head on the table. But when she looked closer she could see that Freida's eyes were wide open, and staring emptily at the wall across from her. Vicky realized that the woman was not sick or sleeping, she was dead.

"She was like this when I came in. I just found her this way. I was just going to collect her dinner tray," Monica rambled, repeating the same statements again and again as Vicky looked at Freida. Vicky knew she was in shock. Vicky was in shock, too. Sarah stepped in behind them. When she saw Freida's body she gasped.

"It's okay, Monica." Sarah wrapped an arm around the woman's shaking shoulders. "It's going to be okay." She nodded to Vicky over Monica's shoulder.

"Sarah, you call 911 and I'll call Mitchell," Vicky suggested. Sarah nodded in agreement as she pulled out her cell phone.

Vicky's finger shook as she selected Mitchell's name on her cell phone. She still didn't quite believe what she was seeing.

"Hello?"

"Mitchell, one of our guests is dead." Vicky grimaced at the admission. She was greeted by a moment of silence as Mitchell grappled with his own shock.

"What? Are you sure?" Mitchell's voice rose with urgency.

"I'm very sure, Sarah is calling 911." Vicky tried to keep her tone from biting, but she was impatient. "But I need your help, Mitchell."

"I know, I'm sorry. I am waiting to give evidence at court, but I'll send someone out now. Do you know who the person is?" Vicky could hear him cover the mouthpiece of the phone. She heard muffled commands. She knew that he was dispatching help.

"Yes. It's Freida Frans." Vicky gulped as she realized the impact of what she had just said. It was bad enough to have someone die at the inn, but this wasn't just anyone. Freida was practically a celebrity. When the media found out, there was going to be quite a lot of curious press to deal with. Vicky didn't want to think about the hassle when she was still standing next to the woman's dead body. She might have been a troublemaker, but she was also a person who had a family, and now she was gone. Vicky felt a little guilty for the way she and Freida had interacted. Much to her shame, she also felt a little relieved. At least she didn't have to worry about a fiercely negative article popping up. There would be plenty of negative media attention surrounding Freida's death, however.

"Sarah, we better make sure that the doors are locked downstairs. Let the staff know not to answer any reporter's questions," Vicky rattled off the instructions while her stomach churned uneasily.

"What about Freida?" Sarah asked. Monica still wept quietly on Sarah's shoulder.

"I'll stay with her." Vicky nodded towards the door. "Make sure that no one finds out about this just yet. We have to treat the situation with respect, and we don't want the press blowing this up before we have the chance to contact Freida's family."

"Good point." Sarah looked at Monica. "Do you think you can walk on your own?"

Monica nodded. She sniffled as she stood to her full height. "I'm sorry."

"You didn't do anything wrong, Monica." Vicky met her eyes with sympathy. "She must have been in poor health."

"Maybe. But she wasn't sick yesterday. When I was putting flowers in her room, she seemed just fine. I don't know how someone can go from being just fine to dead in such a short period of time."

"It is shocking. It's possible that she had some underlying illness. Something that she didn't even know about." Vicky shook her head. She crouched down beside Freida's body. It was such a strange position to die in. It looked as if she had just taken a bite of her food when she simply slumped over into her dinner. Vicky was unsettled by the woman's empty stare. The fruit basket that Vicky had asked Monica to deliver the day before was sitting on the table next to her.

"Come with me, Monica." Sarah steered her out the door.

Once Vicky was alone with Freida, she felt her heart sink. She remembered the phone call that she had overheard. To think that she had been so concerned about Roman Blade without ever knowing that her life was nearing an end. There was nothing to indicate how she had died. Her face was pale, her skin was cold. Otherwise, she appeared to be perfectly fine. There wasn't a trace of blood or a hint of a fight. Vicky looked up when she heard someone walk in the door.

She expected it to be the paramedics, but instead it was Blake, the new bellboy. He stood frozen in the doorway of the room. His eyes widened with horror at the sight of the dead body. Vicky was sure it was the first time he had ever seen one.

"Blake, you shouldn't be here." Vicky frowned. "Please go downstairs and see if Sarah needs any help."

Blake only continued to stare, as if in a trance, at Freida's body.

"Blake!" Vicky raised her voice slightly to try to break him out of the dazed state that he was in. "Please, go see if Sarah needs help with Monica."

"Is she really dead?" Blake was finally able to speak.

"Yes, Blake. But we need to keep that under wraps for now. If it gets out, then her family won't be notified of her death before it ends up on the news. Understand?" She narrowed her eyes.

"Her family," Blake repeated. "Wow." He shook his head. Vicky could see that he was not processing the situation very well. She cleared her throat and stood up. As she walked towards the door she placed a hand on Blake's shoulder. She turned him around towards the hallway.

"You're not helping me here, Blake. I need you to do what you can to help Sarah."

Blake nodded slowly. "Of course. Anything I can do." As he began going down the hallway Vicky caught sight of the paramedics approaching. Vicky gestured to them.

"In here," she kept her voice soft. She didn't want to alert the other guests to what was happening. It was nearly impossible to keep the kind of secret that she was trying to, but she was putting in her best effort. The paramedics eased Freida's body out of the chair and onto the floor. They checked her vitals. Vicky wasn't surprised when they declared the woman dead on arrival. She assumed that Freida had been dead since the night before. As the paramedics prepared her body for the coroner, some officers arrived. After they had spoken to the paramedics one of them swept the plate of food into one zip lock bag and the basket of fruit into another. Vicky was surprised by this.

"What are you doing?" she asked.

The officer looked up at her. "In a case where there is an unknown cause of death, we keep whatever food or drink is nearby. The death appears to be natural, but they're considered potential toxins until the cause of death is determined."

Vicky raised an eyebrow. She had never heard of that before. She saw no reason to protest. "Anything you need to find out what happened," she said. She doubted that the food had anything to do with Freida's death, but she wanted to cooperate. She stepped out of the room to wait for the coroner's van to arrive. Sarah met her in the hallway.

"We're going to have to say something to the guests." Sarah frowned. "They are going to see the gurney and the van."

"Yes, we better be prepared."

"What are you thinking?" Sarah asked.

Vicky rubbed her hands slowly along the smooth surface of her pants. She was trying to get her palms to stop sweating. The more she wiped them, the more they seemed to sweat.

"We'll just stick to what we know. Some of the guests won't see what's happening. For the ones that ask we'll let them know that someone has passed away." Vicky lowered her voice slightly. "We don't know anything else at this point, do we? For all we know she could have overdosed on some drugs."

"Yes, you're right," Sarah agreed.

"Okay, so if you can man the front desk to field questions, I'll wait here by Freida's room in case anyone needs anything." Vicky tilted her head towards the end of the hallway. "Trevor is out walking, but you might want to stop by Roman's room and let him know what is happening. He will want a heads up if any media shows up about this."

"You don't think he'd try to spin it into some kind of campaign promotion do you?" Sarah scrunched up her nose with disgust at the idea.

"I don't know, but I think it's best we warn him." Vicky looked towards the closed door of the room that she knew Roman was staying in. She was surprised that all of the commotion hadn't drawn him out of his room already. Thinking of that, made her wonder where Ida was. She was always the first to show up when there was drama. Hadn't she heard the scream?

"Can you handle it, Vicky?" Sarah asked.

"Sure, of course." Vicky nodded. Sarah headed off down the hallway. Vicky nervously walked up to the door. She hadn't really spoken directly to Roman Blade since he had arrived. She was used to dealing with the wealthy, and even some celebrities, but this was the man who, if elected, would be making decisions for their entire state. She walked up to the door and knocked lightly, twice.

As she waited for an answer, she caught sight of something fluorescent yellow out of the corner of her eye. She turned her attention fully to it and discovered that it was Ida dressed in the brightest jogging outfit that Vicky had ever seen. Right by her side was Roman Blade, dressed in a much more conservative, navy blue jogging suit.

"Aunt Ida." Vicky hurried to her side. "Were you two out jogging this morning?"

"Yes." Ida looked at her with concern. "I saw the coroner's van pull up. What's happened?"

Vicky looked from her aunt, to the man standing beside her. She didn't think about it, she just blurted out the truth.

"Freida Frans is dead." She stared at Roman. "We found her this morning."

"Oh no!" Ida clasped a hand over her mouth in shock. Roman returned Vicky's steady stare.

"How did she die?" he asked.

Vicky was a little startled by the question. It wasn't what she was expecting from him.

"We're not sure. But most likely from natural causes." Vicky continued to study Roman intently. "I thought you should know, in case there is any media attention."

"Good thinking." He nodded. He flashed her a brief presidential smile. "I'd better call Trevor and let him know."

"Let him know what?" Trevor asked as he walked down the hallway towards them.

"Oh Trevor, just who I wanted to see." Trevor looked at Roman with a puzzled expression. "Freida Frans is dead."

"What?" Trevor grew pale. He moved out of the way as the fruit basket and food were carried past them. He looked at them with wide eyes.

"Come to my room so we can discuss this." As they walked away from Ida, Vicky watched them enter Roman's room. When she turned back Ida was peering into Freida's room.

"How awful," she sighed.

"It is." Vicky frowned. "Sarah is not taking it well."

"Of course not." Ida swept her hand back through her hair and pulled off her bright yellow headband. "Poor Freida. It's so shocking when someone in the prime of their life suddenly passes."

"It is." Vicky nodded.

Vicky stepped aside as Freida's body was wheeled out of her room. She was relieved that there were no guests out in the hall to see it. The officers followed behind her.

"Just a precaution in case this wasn't a natural death," one of the officers said as he put police tape across the door.

"We'd better take a quick look at the room, make sure everything is in order," Ida spoke casually once the officers were out of earshot. Vicky couldn't help but smile a little. She knew that her aunt wanted to get into the room and snoop around a bit. She didn't see anything wrong with it either. She had been too shocked to take a good look. Although, it was very likely that Freida had passed from natural causes, it wouldn't hurt to take a look. You never know what you might find.

Chapter Nine

Vicky and Ida pushed aside some of the crime scene tape and stepped inside Freida's room. One of the first things Vicky noticed was the empty food tray on the table. Vicky knew that the food had been collected out of caution, but it still made her a little uneasy. She couldn't imagine taking a bite of food one moment and then dying the next. At least she was certain that Chef Henry's pasta was some of the best that Freida had likely ever eaten.

"Look at this, Vicky." Ida hovered beside the bed.

"What is it?" Vicky joined her. Ida pointed out some papers that were sticking out from under the bed. Vicky found this odd as the staff kept the rooms impeccable, and that included under the bed. Ida crouched down and pulled the papers out. They were crumpled up. Ida handed one of the papers to Vicky and began smoothing out the other one herself. Vicky read over the text on the paper. It seemed to be the introduction of an article.

With the number of lies being bantered about on the campaign trail, please allow me to interject some honesty.

"What does yours say?" Vicky asked. She peered over her aunt's shoulder.

"It's similar, just worded differently. She must have been trying to figure out the best introduction." Ida set the paper down under the bed where she had found it. "I guess this article isn't ever going to see the light of day."

"I guess not." Vicky frowned. A buzzing sound alerted Vicky to a cell phone ringing. She followed the buzzing and crouched down to see the phone on the floor. It had fallen under the bedside table. Vicky picked up the phone nervously. She didn't want to be the one to notify next of kin, but she knew that if she was a friend or family member, she would want to know. The caller ID indicated that it was 'Heather'. She answered the call.

"Hello?" Vicky spoke tentatively.

"I'm sorry I must have dialed the wrong number, I'm trying to reach Freida Frans."

"You have the right number. May I ask who's calling?"

"This is her editor, Heather. Why do you have Freida's phone?" The woman's voice raised with urgency.

Vicky cringed as she knew that there was no easy way to put this. "I'm sorry to tell you this, but Freida passed away this morning." Vicky tried to be as gentle as possible.

"What? Is this some kind of joke?" Heather demanded.

"No, I'm sorry it's not. My name is Vicky, I'm one of the owners of the inn she was staying at. I'm afraid we found her this morning, she had passed away some time during the night." Vicky looked over at Ida who nodded her head in support.

"Oh no! This can't be happening! I knew it! I knew that bastard would kill her!" Heather sounded hysterical. Vicky couldn't understand everything she was saying.

"So far it looks like she died of natural causes, there's no indication of foul play." Vicky tried to get her message across, but Heather had already hung up the phone.

Vicky felt a dull ache begin in the center of her chest. Was Heather the same person that Freida had been on the phone with when she said she wasn't afraid of Roman Blade? Vicky pushed the thought out of her mind. The clearest assumption was that Freida had died of natural causes. She led a very stressful life, and perhaps that stress had finally caught up with her.

"What did she say?" Ida asked. She could tell from Vicky's wide eyes that it had been unexpected.

"She said she knew that bastard would kill her," Vicky explained. "At least that's what I think she said. It was hard to tell as she was so upset."

"We'll know soon enough if there was anything suspicious about her death." Ida sighed. "It looks like there isn't much more to see in here."

"She hadn't even slept in her bed." Vicky looked at the perfectly made bed. "We'd better get downstairs, I have a feeling a few guests are going to want to check out." Vicky headed for the elevator. "We also don't want to be caught in here."

"I'll be right down, I'm just going to change." Ida headed for her room.

Alone in the elevator Vicky thought about the last time she had spoken to Freida. It hadn't been a very pleasant exchange. She wished that she had been a little kinder to the woman. Perhaps she had been too quick to judge her. Just because she promoted gossip, that didn't make her a bad person. As Vicky stepped out of the elevator on the ground floor, she felt an increasing sense of dismay. She didn't want to face the guests who would have plenty of questions.

As she walked out into the lobby she noticed there were a few people milling about. They seemed to be watching the coroner's van and gossiping to each other. Vicky caught sight of Monica sitting at a table outside. She was stirring a cup of coffee and staring at the table. Vicky pushed open the glass door and walked quickly over to her.

"Are you doing okay, Monica?" She sat down beside her at the table.

"I don't know." Monica shook her head. "I just can't believe this."

"Maybe you should go home." Vicky offered the suggestion gently. "You've had quite a shock."

"No, it's better if I keep working." Monica winced. "Trust me."

Vicky raised an eyebrow. "Is something wrong at home, Monica?"

"No, it's just I'm so tired, and the baby is very clingy. I think it would just be better if I stayed until I was in a better state of mind." Monica finally took a sip of her coffee.

"All right. Whatever feels right to you." Vicky gave Monica's hand a light squeeze. She remembered how difficult it was for Sarah with two young kids. The infant stage could be trying at times.

"Thanks, Vicky." Monica grasped her cup of coffee tightly. "I just keep thinking about that poor woman. Maybe if I had just..."

"There is nothing that you could have done, Monica." Vicky met her eyes with a sympathetic smile. "This was in no way your fault."

Monica looked back at her with a guilty frown. "I guess you're right." She looked past Vicky towards the front desk. "It looks like someone needs you."

Vicky turned to see a couple waiting impatiently at the front desk. "Okay. Let me know if you need anything."

"Thanks, Vicky." Monica took another sip of her coffee.

Vicky walked inside and over to the front desk. She put on her most pleasant expression and prepared for the worst.

"How can I help you?" she asked.

"We would like to check out." The woman smacked her room key down on the desk. Vicky jumped a little at the sharp sound.

"I understand. This morning's events were disturbing." Vicky used the room number to pull up the identity of the couple. The room was registered under Chandler Millers. "I'll get you checked out as quickly as possible."

"We aren't leaving because of that," the woman said with a snooty tone to her voice. "People die you know. That's just a thing of life. But I can't believe that you would allow such people to stay in your inn." She raised her nose into the air.

"What?" Vicky was confused. "Who do you mean?"

"I mean that scoundrel, Roman Blade, everyone knows that he is a common criminal. Allowing him to stay here with his deceitful campaign manager is like promoting him and his campaign. When I heard that he was staying here I told my Chandler that we had to go right away."

Chandler, who had yet to speak, lowered his eyes. Vicky grimaced. "We haven't endorsed anyone for governor." Vicky did her best to explain in a neutral tone.

"Like I said, renting him a room is the same as endorsing him. We will not stand for it."

Vicky narrowed her eyes. "How do you know that he's a criminal?"

"I can read, can't I?" She laughed. She signed the receipt that Vicky handed her. "In fact I read all about the way he covered up his criminal activity. We don't need more liars in positions of power, now do we?"

Vicky thought that she was being very harsh. But she knew that there were many people who were very passionate about the politicians they supported. She had no idea that Roman was such a controversial figure, but that would not have stopped him from being able to stay at the inn. Sarah and Vicky agreed that it wasn't their place to judge a guest.

"Well, I'm sorry that we couldn't continue to accommodate you." Vicky handed them a business card. "If you'd like to stay with us in the future, please feel free to contact us at any time."

"Hmph, I don't see that happening." The woman marched away from the front desk. Her husband trailed quietly after her. Vicky looked at them with dismay as she watched them go.

As she finished typing their reason for leaving in the records on the computer, her cell phone began to ring. She reached into her pocket and pulled it out. She could see that it was Mitchell calling. She smiled at the thought of hearing his voice.

"Hello?"

"Vicky, I've got something I have to tell you." Mitchell rushed forward without even greeting her. Vicky knew instantly that it must be serious.

"What is it?" She listened closely.

"I just spoke with the coroner." Mitchell's voice was weighted with concern.

"What is it?" she asked again. "Not natural causes I guess?"

"No. It's worse than that. Freida was poisoned."

"Oh no! That's horrible." Vicky grimaced as she wondered who would do such a terrible thing. "I guess the police will have to investigate. How was she poisoned?"

"Vicky, Freida was killed by ingesting poisonous berries." Mitchell paused a moment as the revelation sunk in. "They were in the fruit basket."

"No," Vicky said with disbelief. "How terrible!"

"Do you know where the fruit came from?"

"No idea, I found the basket on the front desk." Vicky sighed with dread as she realized that the fruit basket she had asked Monica to deliver to the room had killed Freida. "Monica delivered it. I asked her to."

"That's strange!" Mitchell exclaimed. "The card that came with the basket said 'With Compliments from the Management of the Heavenly Highland Inn. Sorry for any inconvenience caused by the disruption to dinner service.'"

"That's impossible," Vicky gasped. "We never arranged any fruit baskets for the guests."

"Maybe Sarah..."

"No," Vicky cut him off. "The basket was delivered to the inn. It had a room number and the address of the inn on the delivery slip."

"Where's the delivery slip?" Mitchell asked.

"We would have thrown it out already."

"I'll get the officers to see if they can find it in the trash."

"I'll double check the trash can, but I'm sure it's been emptied, the trash was collected this morning." Vicky cringed.

"So, you have no idea who the basket of fruit came from?"

"No," Vicky said slowly. "I'll try to find out, though." Her heart began to pound harder.

"You need to leave this to the police! You can expect that there is going to be a thorough investigation. Someone put those berries in the fruit basket. I'm sure it was an accident. But it's led to someone's death so we are going to have to find out what happened."

"I understand," Vicky murmured. She could barely catch enough of a breath to speak at a normal level. Finding Freida dead was shocking enough, but to find out that she was poisoned by fruit apparently given to her as a gift from the inn was very upsetting, not to mention confusing.

"I'll update you as much as I can, Vicky. Just be careful what you say and to whom, until all of this is settled. Okay?" She could tell by the tone of his voice that he expected an actual answer.

"Of course," Vicky stated without conviction.

"Vicky, we're sending out some officers to look into the situation more. I will be there as soon as I can. But whatever they ask you to do, you need to do. Showing cooperation will make things easier on the inn." His voice hardened slightly. Vicky didn't appreciate the commanding tone.

"I have to do what I have to do to protect my staff and the reputation of the inn, Mitchell. You and I both know that cooperation can sometimes lead to a false arrest, and statements being used against people." Vicky sighed. She knew that she was taking her frustration and fear out on Mitchell, and that wasn't fair. "I'm sure all of this will turn out to be some terrible mistake."

"I'm sure it will, too. I'll be there as soon as I can. All right?" His voice was warm with sympathy.

"All right. Thanks, Mitchell." When Vicky hung up the phone she felt her heart sink. She knew that Mitchell had asked her to stay out of the investigation, but she needed to know the truth. She thought she would start by seeing if she could find out where the fruit was from.

When she reached the door to the kitchen, Sarah was there.

"How is everything going?" Sarah asked. Then she noticed Vicky's grim expression. "What's wrong?"

"Did you arrange for a fruit basket to be delivered to Freida from the inn?"

"No," Sarah replied with a puzzled expression. "Why?"

"I just spoke to Mitchell," Vicky explained gently. "The news isn't good."

"What is it?" Sarah asked with urgency.

"The coroner found the cause of Freida's death. Poisonous berries, which were found in the fruit basket delivered to her room. Apparently, they were delivered with the compliments of the management of the Heavenly Highland Inn."

"What?" Sarah's eyes flew wide open. "That can't be! How is that possible?"

"I don't know, but the police found the note and the berries with the fruit that were in the basket," Vicky explained. "Mitchell said that some officers will be here soon to start an investigation."

"Unbelievable," Sarah groaned. "This is terrible. That poor woman lost her life, and the inn is going to lose its good reputation."

"Mitchell said to cooperate with the police, but it seems as if someone might be trying to frame us and I think we need to be very careful what we say."

"You're right." Sarah nodded. She rubbed her cheeks in slow circles with her palms. Vicky could tell that she was close to exploding. She couldn't even reassure her, because she was feeling the same way.

"I'd better call our lawyer." Sarah frowned. "We need to know how to protect ourselves in this situation."

"I'll talk to Chef Henry and Aunt Ida to make sure they didn't arrange the basket. Let me know what the lawyer says." Vicky started to turn away, then paused. "Sarah, we're going to figure this out. Everything is going to be fine."

Sarah raised an eyebrow. "That's what you said about the banquet hall."

"I know, I know." Vicky sighed and headed for the kitchen.

Chapter Ten

When Vicky walked into the kitchen, she noticed right away that Henry was doing his inventory. He had several boxes pulled out of the pantry and a clipboard in his hand. Sarah had offered several times to arrange for another staff member to do that for him so he could focus on cooking, but he was very picky about his food and preferred to keep track of it himself.

"Chef Henry." Vicky's voice trembled slightly as she spoke. Henry glanced over at her swiftly and then back at his clipboard.

"Please, give me just a moment, Vicky, or I will lose track of my count." He turned back to the crate of tomatoes he was sorting through. Vicky waited patiently. It was not as if waiting a few more minutes was going to change what had already happened.

"I'm sorry to make you wait, Vicky. The inventory should have been done yesterday, but with everything that happened I didn't have the chance to complete it. The delivery driver put the food away for me yesterday because I had to leave suddenly to turn off the water when the sprinkler broke. He had the best intentions, but he put it away in the wrong places of course." He sighed. "Now, everything is taking longer than usual and I'm running behind and I would hate to have to start all over again." He looked at her with a flustered expression.

"I understand." Vicky nodded. "Henry, I have to tell you something. I want you to understand that I am in no way accusing you, but we need to prepare for an investigation."

Henry narrowed his eyes as he tried to figure out what she meant. "What are you talking about, Vicky?"

"Did you organize a fruit basket for Freida's room by any chance?" Vicky asked gently.

"No," Henry said as he shook his head. "Why?"

"It looks like Freida didn't die of natural causes. She had fruit delivered to her room with a card saying it was from the inn. There were poisonous berries in the fruit basket." Vicky frowned.

"Well, they didn't come from this kitchen, we don't have any berries here," Henry said defensively. "They aren't in season at the moment."

"Okay," Vicky said. "Where would someone get a fruit basket around here?"

"The first place that comes to mind in Highland is the grocers, but they could have come from anywhere."

"I know." Vicky sighed. "But it's the best place to start. No one organized the basket at the inn so..."

"Well, that's good to know." A police officer walked into the kitchen just as Vicky was finishing her statement. Vicky presumed he must be one of the new officers in Highland because she hadn't met him before. "I would like to ask some questions about..."

"We don't have any statements to make at this time," Vicky blurted out before thinking. She didn't want to give a statement when it looked like the inn could have been negligent by sending the poisonous berries to the room.

The officer looked at Vicky with disdain. "I'm assuming that your tune will change when your husband gets here."

Vicky narrowed her eyes. "Not necessarily."

"Right, well we need to investigate this thoroughly," he said. "If that means I need to shut down the inn to do that, I will," he threatened.

Vicky was stunned by his rude demeanor. She read his name tag.

"Officer Barlett, is it?" She raised an eyebrow. "I wonder if your supervisor is aware of the way you treat people?"

"He's very aware of the way I treat people who refuse to cooperate with an investigation." Officer Barlett straightened his shoulders. "Now, would you like to give me a statement about those berries?"

"Excuse me, Sir, but that is no way to talk..." Henry began to say. Vicky interrupted him.

"No, Henry, let him be." She gestured to the officer. "Are we done here?"

Officer Barlett glowered at her but nodded. "For the moment." He turned and walked away.

"Thank you for your support, Henry," Vicky said.

"Let's just hope this is sorted out soon."

"I hope so," Vicky replied as she turned and walked out of the kitchen.

***

Vicky was troubled as she went to find Sarah. She knew that she should have been a little kinder to the officer, especially since Mitchell would likely hear about it, but she was on the defensive, and she was very worried about the future of the inn.

Sarah was just hanging up her phone behind the front desk. She turned to face Vicky with a stricken look.

"Our lawyer says not to say a word." Sarah blinked back tears. "Vicky, I don't think that we're going to get out of this one. We're going to have to start thinking about what we're going to do."

"Sarah, try not to stress too much," Vicky urged. She hated to see her sister so worried, though she understood why she was. "I'm going to figure out what happened. Chef Henry says the berries could not have come from his kitchen."

"Good, that's a start," Sarah said. "But who sent the basket."

"I don't know, but I'm going to try to find out," she said with determination. "I'm first going to check that Aunt Ida didn't organize the basket, then I'm going to start with the grocers to see if they know who could have ordered it."

Sarah nodded vaguely. "I better make a few more calls."

As she disappeared inside the office, Vicky felt her stomach flip. Things were about to go from bad to worse, and if she didn't find out the truth fast, her family might just lose everything.

"Vicky?" Ida walked up to her. "What's going on?"

"Aunt Ida," Vicky said. "Where have you been?"

"I just went for a walk."

"Did you organize a basket of fruit to be delivered to Freida?" Vicky asked before explaining anything.

"No, of course not," Ida said with confusion. "Why?"

"I'll explain on the way. We need to take a trip, Aunt Ida." Vicky looked at her aunt. "There's no time to waste."

Chapter Eleven

On the drive to the grocery store Vicky filled Ida in on the poisonous berries. Ida's expression grew more and more grave with everything that Vicky said. By the time they parked, Ida was just as determined as Vicky.

"We have to find out who did this." Ida stepped out of the car. Vicky did as well.

"I know!" Vicky held the door of the store open for Ida and then followed her inside. The small grocery store was one of the locally owned businesses that the inn used. It might have been a little cheaper for them to use a larger grocery store from a neighboring town for their supplies, but they felt the investment in the community was worth the extra cost, especially seeing as the store sourced its fresh ingredients locally wherever possible. A man stood behind the counter near the deli. He wore a white apron. His short, black hair was receding in a half moon from his forehead. His cheeks were round and full.

"Excuse me?" Vicky walked towards the counter. The moon looked up at her. Vicky recognized him as John, the owner of the grocery store.

"Hi, Vicky, Ida." He greeted them with a smile. "How are you today?" He turned fully to face them. Vicky noticed that there were several bins of fresh fruit nearby.

"Not the best, John," Vicky replied.

"We have had an incident with someone at the inn." Ida sprang forward with an explanation before Vicky could continue. Vicky knew that it was because Ida was more of the charmer.

"Oh? It's not Henry I hope?" He stepped around the counter towards them.

"No, one of the guests was delivered a fruit basket yesterday," Ida explained. "Did anyone order a fruit basket from you yesterday?"

"I don't think so," he said thoughtfully. "But I didn't work all day yesterday."

"Is there any way you can check, please?" Ida asked.

"Sure." He walked over to the computer and tapped a few keys. "Yes, there were a couple of fruit baskets ordered yesterday." Vicky tried not to show any reaction as she didn't want him to stop giving them information. And she had a feeling he would stop if he knew the severity of what had occurred.

"Can you tell who ordered them please?" Ida asked hopefully.

John tapped a few more keys and then shook his head. "No, I can't. They both paid cash and took them with them. I wasn't working, but I can call Lukey and see if he remembers."

"Thank you," Ida said. Vicky and Ida exchanged a nervous glance as John picked up the phone. He dialed the number and then waited.

"He's not picking up." He shook his head and hung up. "He's going on vacation today, but I can try get hold of him later."

"Can you call us when you get hold of him, please?" Ida asked with a smile.

"Of course," John replied.

"Thank you," Ida said.

"What's all of this about, anyway?"

Ida hesitated and then began explaining "There were poisonous berries in the basket." Ida met his eyes directly. "The recipient passed away."

"Poisonous berries?" he gasped. "But how?"

"We presume they must have been put in the basket by mistake," Vicky explained.

The man stared at her with a mixture of shock and concern. "Are you trying to say that you think I provided the poisonous berries?" He looked from Vicky to Ida, who he seemed to think was more reasonable. "That's not possible!"

"How isn't it possible?" Vicky asked. "If the berries were in the basket and the basket came from your store."

"No!" the grocer said with conviction. "They did not come from my store. Why would I deal in poisonous berries?" He shook his head. "I don't stock berries at the moment at all. The varieties grown locally aren't in season and I only stock what's in season. Have a look for yourself," he said as he gestured to the crates of fruit.

"Okay." All of the vigor had left Vicky's voice as she ran her eyes over all the fruit. There were no berries in sight. She felt even more confused than she had been when she first arrived.

"Thanks for your time." Ida smiled. "Please let us know if you get hold of Lukey."

"I will." John nodded, but he wasn't smiling.

"We should go," Ida whispered to Vicky.

"All right." Vicky didn't really want to leave. She didn't want to walk out of the grocery store with no idea of what had happened to Freida. She didn't want to have to go back to Sarah with even more confusion. Where did the berries come from?

As her aunt stepped out the door, Vicky followed after her. She had convinced herself the berries had come from the grocer. Now there was no proof of that. Still, Vicky questioned whether the grocer was telling the truth. Had he slipped some berries into the order and then found out that they were poisonous and thrown them away? Had he put them in there by mistake? Or worse, had he added them on purpose?

Ida started the car, but before she backed out of the parking space she turned to look at Vicky.

"You look so upset, sweetheart." She frowned. "What's going on in your head?"

Vicky exhaled and felt as if she was ready to explode. "If the berries didn't come from the grocery store then where did they come from? If they weren't in the fruit basket when it was prepared then how did they get in?"

"That's presuming that the basket that was delivered was from the grocers," Ida reminded her.

"I know," Vicky admitted. "But how will we ever find out where the fruit basket came from if it wasn't from the grocers. It is very annoying."

"Oh, I see." Ida nodded. "You're right, that is frustrating. Maybe we need to stop chasing the fruit for a bit, and focus instead on who might have wanted Freida dead."

"I have a feeling it is not going to be a very short list."

Chapter Twelve

As soon as Ida and Vicky returned to the inn, Vicky headed straight for her apartment. Ida was right on her heels.

"What's the plan?" Ida asked.

"The plan is to hunt down the truth about what Freida was up to, and who her enemies were." Vicky opened the door to the apartment and rushed inside. She moved so fast that she nearly collided with Mitchell who was turning to face her. "Oops. Sorry, Mitchell." She took a slight step back. When she saw Mitchell's expression she was glad she did. He did not look very pleased to see her.

"I was looking for you." His voice was even as he settled his gaze upon her.

"I'll just be out here." Ida avoided entering the apartment. Vicky slowly closed the door behind her.

"Well, here I am." She smiled at him.

"Can I ask you why it is that you told my officer that he couldn't question you?" Mitchell frowned.

"Your officer?" Vicky stared at him for a moment. "Mitchell, are you the investigating detective on this case?"

"Not exactly." He cleared his throat. "There is quite a conflict of interest, so another detective was assigned the case, but I have asked him to keep me in the loop. I did that to make sure that you and Sarah would be treated fairly. However, I didn't expect you not to offer the same courtesy to me."

"First of all your officer was rude to me." Vicky crossed her arms. "Secondly, we have to cover ourselves legally, Mitchell. If we give interviews, that could be used against us later."

"Only if you are guilty." Mitchell studied her. "Are you more concerned about protecting the inn or finding the truth about a woman's death?"

His words hit home with Vicky. She wanted to protest against the accusation, but she couldn't.

She had been more focused on figuring out where the berries had come from and how they ended up in a basket in Freida's room that was supposedly organized by the inn than she had been about Freida being dead.

"Listen, Mitchell. I went to see the grocer and he says that there were two fruit baskets ordered yesterday, but they have no details of who ordered them and they don't have any berries in stock at all. I'm starting to think that maybe someone added the berries to the order afterwards. I think this has all been intentional and the fact that it was addressed from the inn makes it even worse."

"I know," Mitchell said. "That is why you need to give your statements. You need to look like you are cooperating with the investigation, and I won't have to face an inquisition about why my wife is stalling a police investigation." He reached out and took her hand in his. "I understand why you don't always trust the police, but I'm your husband. I know you trust me."

Vicky nodded silently. She knew that she could trust him. She also knew that he was right, stalling the investigation would only make them look guiltier in the eyes of the law.

"Don't ever think that we can be on opposite sides, Vicky. I will always be in your corner."

Vicky felt some relief at his words. After Mitchell left the apartment, Ida stepped inside.

"What was all of that about?" she asked.

"It was about the berries of course, but it's nothing to worry about. Now, let's find out why Freida might have been a target." She opened up her computer and began searching. Ida peered over her shoulder as Vicky brought up article after article and skimmed over them. Most of them were junk stories, but some seemed to have a newsworthy cause.

"I'll get us some coffee." Ida walked towards the kitchen.

The more Vicky looked at Freida's articles the more she began to suspect that Freida was more of a skilled journalist than she often portrayed herself to be.

"Have you found anything yet?" Ida walked over with two cups of coffee from the kitchen.

"I might have." Vicky frowned. "But I don't think you're going to like it."

"What is it?" Ida asked.

"It looks like Freida was working hard to expose the truth about the war injury that Roman claims. She was publishing articles about how no evidence could be found to prove that he had even been in a war, let alone injured in one." Vicky frowned as she read over the information.

"I remember him telling me about that during our walk." Ida grimaced. "That would be a terrible thing to lie about. I definitely think he has an injury."

"But was it caused in a war?" Vicky asked. "I bet Freida had finally found proof and she was going to reveal it. I overheard her saying she was not afraid of Roman. I wonder if he had been threatening her in an attempt to cover up the information she found. He might have been the person who her editor was talking about on the phone."

"Roman doesn't seem very threatening." Ida shook her head. "He seems more like he would be a caring and determined leader."

"Aunt Ida, I respect your opinion, but don't all politicians try to be perceived that way?" Vicky felt a little bad for questioning her aunt. She knew that Ida had a lot more experience than she did when it came to world travels and different political customs, but to her it seemed as if her aunt had allowed herself to be caught up in something that wasn't quite true.

"You might be right about that," Ida reluctantly agreed. She didn't want to admit that she might have been conned. "He does seem like a nice fellow though."

"But we need to find out if that nice fellow committed murder." Vicky tapped her finger lightly against the keyboard. "I'm going to call her editor and see what information she had about Roman. Maybe if we know exactly what it was she had found, we'll get a lead."

"Maybe." Ida grew quiet. Vicky knew she was upset by the idea that Roman might be involved. But the more Vicky thought about it, the more sense it made to her. Roman obviously was hoping for a big political future, if Freida had found something that would end that, before it even had the chance to properly get off the ground, he might be angry enough to eliminate her. Vicky decided to take a walk while she made the call.

"I'm going to get some fresh air, Aunt Ida. Do you want to join me?" Vicky asked.

"No, I think I'm going to scrounge up something to eat." Ida left Vicky's apartment with a smile on her lips, but Vicky could tell she was faking it. It bothered Vicky to suspect someone who Ida was so certain was innocent, but she felt her aunt was dazzled by Roman's charm. She had jotted down Heather's number earlier. She rummaged in her purse to find it, then dialed it on her cell phone. As she stepped outside she was greeted by cool, crisp air. As the evening progressed, the temperature was steadily dropping.

"Hello?" Heather sounded exhausted.

"Hello, Heather, this is Vicky from the Heavenly Highland Inn."

"Oh yes, Vicky. I've already spoken to the police and the coroner."

"I understand. I was just thinking about what you said earlier, and I was wondering if there was anything more you could tell me. Or maybe what Freida was working on," Vicky paused. She wondered if Heather would be willing to tell her anything.

"Why do you want to know?" There was hesitation in Heather's voice. "Do you work for them?"

"Them? Who do you mean?" Vicky sat down in the patio area outside the banquet hall.

"Roman Blade and Trevor Scales."

"Of course not. They are staying at the inn though. Is that who you think hurt Freida?" Vicky's heart skipped a beat. "Is it because of something she found out about Roman?"

"What does it matter now? She's gone."

"That doesn't mean that someone shouldn't be punished if they murdered her," Vicky pointed out.

"Listen, the coroner told me that her food was poisoned. The police are acting like your inn might be responsible for her death. So, why are you talking to me?"

"I know it wasn't our fault. I know that someone sent the fruit basket to frame us. I'm just trying to figure out why, and who." Vicky sighed. "Maybe it was a mistake to call."

"Look, I was upset earlier. Yes, Freida was investigating Roman, and yes, she had some dirt on him and was digging for more. But that doesn't make him a killer. I think you need to worry about what's happening in your kitchen. Trust me, you don't want to make an enemy out of Roman Blade and his entourage." With that she hung up. Vicky listened to the resulting dial tone for a few moments before hanging up as well.

Had Heather just warned her not to look into Roman? Vicky had always trusted her aunt's judgment before. Maybe not her fashion sense, but Ida always had a pretty good grasp on people. Could she really be this wrong about Roman? Vicky sighed as she wondered if she had been too caught up in the idea that Roman was guilty. She decided to head inside and go over other possible suspects. Vicky walked past the windows of the banquet hall. She had her mind on what might have really happened to Freida. Was it really possible that someone had intentionally poisoned her? If so, was it Roman or Trevor? Was it someone on the staff? It made her feel terrible to even consider it. It could have been anyone really.

As Vicky turned towards the banquet hall to head back inside she noticed a shadow moving through it. The banquet hall had been closed since Freida's body had been found. Vicky was certain that no one should be inside. Her stomach tightened. Was someone trying to repeat the event, perhaps with a new target?

Vicky crept close to the windows. She didn't want to alert whoever was inside to the fact that she was on to them. Instead she wanted to catch them in the act. Vicky saw the shadow move across the wall again. It was very large and rotund. In fact it reminded her of a bear. At that thought her chest grew tight. She recalled thinking the same thing about the plumber. Was it Benny inside? Had he been the one to poison Freida? Vicky shuddered at the idea. She had no idea why Benny would want Freida dead. She knew that he didn't have much business, had he broken the sprinkler head hoping to get himself a job? It didn't make much sense to Vicky, but there he was lumbering through the banquet hall.

Vicky grabbed the handle of the side door of the hall and pulled it open slowly and silently.

Benny continued towards the double doors at the entrance. Vicky slipped into the banquet hall behind him.

"Just what do you think you're doing?" she commanded. She was terrified on the inside, but she wanted to seem intimidating on the outside. Benny turned around slowly to face her. He stared at her through dim lighting.

"You have something of mine." He narrowed his eyes.

"What is that supposed to mean?" Vicky demanded.

Benny took a large step towards her. Vicky was surprised by how much space he could cover with one outstretched leg.

"Just what it means. I came back for my fans." He met her eyes. "Remember? I let you use them to dry the carpet. I need them back. There was no one in the lobby and I thought they might be in here."

"Oh, that's the reason why you were roaming around here in the dark?" Vicky was still skeptical.

"I couldn't figure out how to turn the lights on. You know I did you a favor by leaving those fans in the first place. Maybe you could be kind enough to return them?" He scowled at her.

Vicky found that his story was beginning to add up. He did have a reason for being there. As far as she had seen he had not even attempted to enter the kitchen.

"Of course, I'm sorry. I didn't mean to accuse you." She sighed. "The fans are in the storage closet in the hallway. Follow me."

She stepped past him. He trailed after her.

"I can see why you're jumpy. Did you figure out who damaged the sprinkler?"

"No." Vicky opened the door to the storage closet. "I haven't really thought about it to be honest."

She frowned as he retrieved his fans. Now that he had reminded her of the sprinkler head, it made her wonder. Had the person who damaged the sprinkler been somehow connected to the murder? Did someone do this to damage the reputation of the inn? Or was there another connection?

"Thanks for helping me get these. Remember me for any future plumbing needs." He flashed her a smile.

"I will." Vicky was distracted as she closed the closet door. As she began walking down the hallway she recalled how the entire cause of the chaotic dinner was the flooded banquet hall. Would someone really go to such lengths to stage enough of a diversion to create a reason to send the fruit basket as an apology from management and poison Freida? The thought of it made Vicky cringe. It also made her even more worried that the murderer might just be someone on the inn's staff. She turned on her heel and headed back into the banquet hall. She needed to try and find out if a staff member was responsible for poisoning Freida.

Chapter Thirteen

As Vicky walked through the banquet hall into the kitchen, the door to the courtyard opened at the same time. Ida stepped in and met Vicky's eyes.

"What are you doing here?" she asked.

"I'm guessing the same thing that you are." Vicky smiled a little. "I was going to go through the events of last night to see who could have put the berries in the basket after it was delivered."

"Yes, we are definitely here for the same reason."

Vicky was often surprised at how similar she and her aunt thought. It made her proud to think that she took after her aunt in many ways.

"What if whoever broke the sprinkler is also the killer?" Vicky walked around behind the kitchen island. "It might have even been the same person that closed the windows I know I left open. Maybe they're trying to frame us."

"Do you really think the two are connected?" Ida asked dubiously. "If so, that means that someone has been planning this for some time."

"I know, we need to try and piece the events together," Vicky said.

"We know that the basket was delivered by Monica to room 310," Ida said.

"Yes?" Vicky looked towards the voice to see Monica standing in the doorway of the kitchen. "Did you need something, Vicky?"

"Why are you still here?" Vicky asked. Her voice was a little harder than usual.

Monica blushed and looked down at her hands. "I fell asleep. I was changing the linen on a bed in one of the guest rooms. I was so tired. I just wanted to lay down, just for a moment. I know my shift ended hours ago, but I just woke up."

"Monica, I don't care if you took a nap." Vicky felt sympathy for Monica as she could see how tired she was.

"Vicky, you seem upset with me." Monica frowned. "Did I do something wrong?"

"No." Vicky shook her head. "But I have a question for you. When you took the fruit basket to Freida's room did you notice if there were berries in it?" Vicky looked at her intently.

"I can't remember," she admitted. Then she got a bit irate which Vicky presumed was from exhaustion. "I'm sorry, I'm sorry. I'm just so tired. It was such a shock to find her that way. I just can't remember. I thought she had died from natural causes."

"Vicky's not accusing you, Monica," Ida spoke up softly from behind Vicky. "We're just trying to get to the bottom of it all."

"When you left the room did she say anything to you?" Vicky asked.

"No. She didn't even look at me. She was on the phone. So, I just left the fruit." Monica reached up and wiped at her eyes. "Maybe if I had paid more attention somehow this wouldn't have happened."

"Monica, it sounds like you did everything you could." Ida smiled soothingly at the woman. "Why don't you go home and get some rest?"

"If only I could." She sniffled as she left the banquet hall.

Ida turned to face Vicky. "She is so upset."

"I would be, too," Vicky said. "I don't know what would be the best thing to do next."

"Well, we still need to figure out where the berries came from. Maybe if we do some research into where they are sold, or where they can be harvested, we might be able to get a better idea of who had them. We need to find out who had access to the berries and whether they knew they were poisonous and why someone pretended that management delivered the basket," Ida said.

"What about the sprinkler?" Vicky reminded her. "Maybe it has something to do with it as well."

"It could still be a coincidence," Ida suggested.

"No matter what it takes we need to figure this out. Until we know who and why, everyone at the inn might be at risk." Ida nodded with a worried expression. "I'm going to see if Sarah has any new information about the fruit basket," Vicky said.

"Okay, I'll meet up with you later." Ida nodded.

Vicky knew that Sarah had not yet left for the day. She found her near the front desk gathering her purse and jacket.

"I'm going home," she announced her intentions before Vicky could even speak. "The kids are wild, and I'm tired, I need my husband and my kids, and a soft bed."

"I understand," Vicky said sympathetically. "But I need to talk to you about something first."

Sarah looked at her with dread. "What is it? I'm sure that things can't get any worse."

"Not here." Vicky pulled Sarah into the small office behind the front desk. Once inside the office Sarah turned to face her.

"What is it? Did you find out something about Freida's death?" Sarah looked at her sister anxiously.

"It's more than that, Sarah. I think we need to consider that Monica might be involved in this. She did deliver the fruit basket." She knew that she should also tell Sarah about the conversation she had with Heather, and the information she had found out about Roman, but she didn't think that Sarah needed to know all of that just yet.

"Monica wouldn't be involved in something like this."

"But Monica has also been exhausted, Sarah. Maybe she made a mistake. Or maybe someone offered her enough money to take a long vacation." Vicky crossed her arms.

"Vicky, that's terrible!" Sarah shook her head.

"It might be, but let's be honest here, enough money can make people do terrible things. I'm not saying that it wouldn't surprise me if it turns out to be Monica, I never would expect her to do something like that, but still, as of now she was the one with the murder weapon so to speak."

Vicky unfolded her arms and tucked her hands into her pockets. She could tell that Sarah was upset by the very idea of her questioning Monica's involvement, but Vicky also knew that Sarah was extra sympathetic to Monica. Sarah had been where Monica was, exhausted and struggling to stay awake because of a teething baby. Sarah could understand where Monica was coming from. Vicky on the other hand, saw the potential for that exhaustion and desperation to be exploited by someone who wanted to get rid of Freida. Vicky was fairly certain that the woman had no shortage of enemies after all of the scathing articles she had written.

"It would have been a big coincidence that she got to deliver the fruit basket in the first place,"

Sarah said as her cell phone began to ring. She looked at the screen. "It's Phil," she explained to Vicky as she answered. While Sarah spoke to her husband, Vicky glanced around the office. She was starting to feel paranoid about who might have damaged the sprinkler and why. The question in her mind was did Freida die because of something she had done or written, or had she died in an attempt to ruin the reputation of the inn. Her stomach churned with disgust.

As Vicky thought about all the possible scenarios, the same scenario played over in her head as Sarah walked towards her. "Do you think it's possible that Roman ordered the fruit basket?" Vicky asked thoughtfully as soon as Sarah had ended her call.

"But why would he do that?" Sarah met Vicky's eyes.

"Because Freida wouldn't leave him alone." Vicky swallowed thickly as she realized she was going to have to tell Sarah the truth about everything she had witnessed and overheard.

"Freida felt threatened by Roman and visa versa. He didn't want her writing articles about him. Maybe he decided that the best way to control her was to silence her once and for all. There was a lot of bad blood between them." Vicky shuddered at the thought. "Maybe he even hired someone to poison her."

"Vicky, that is a huge accusation to make," Sarah whispered as if she was worried that someone might hear her. "We don't have any proof. How do you know Freida was threatened by him?"

"I overheard her telling her editor on the phone yesterday. Then she tried to catch Aunt Ida and Roman together. And tonight I spoke with her editor, who warned me not to make an enemy out of Roman." Vicky lowered her eyes.

"Vicky, you knew all of this and didn't tell me?" Sarah tightened her lips with impatience. "We're supposed to be a team."

"I know that. I was going to tell you, Sarah."
Vicky looked at her sister pleadingly. "I just didn't
want to upset you more than you already were."

"Look, Vicky, I might be stressed or upset, but
that doesn't mean I can't handle the truth, or
whatever you find out. I need to know that we're
working together, okay?" Sarah looked at her
sister sternly. Vicky recalled that look from many
years of Sarah being the older and wiser sibling.

"Yes, I'm sorry." Vicky frowned.

"Good. Now, what are we going to do about
this?"

"We need to see if it's possible that Roman
ordered the fruit basket."

"But if he did wouldn't he have it delivered to
his room not Freida's so he could put the berries
in first?" Sarah asked. Her suggestion made Vicky
recall the slip that was on the fruit basket. Her
eyes widened at the sudden realization. She was
sure it said room 301 not 310. But could she be
mistaken? She was so tired that night.

Vicky quickly went to the computer and looked up the name of the guest staying in room 301. When she saw the name her heart stopped for a moment. Was this really possible?

"Vicky, what is it?" Sarah asked. She could tell that her sister had stumbled across something unpleasant.

"I think that the fruit basket was meant to be delivered to a different room."

"What?"

"I think that the slip indicating the room number said room 301, Roman's room."

"So where's the slip?" Sarah asked.

"It's been thrown away like we always do."

Vicky's mind quickly ran through the possible repercussions of this discovery. Had Monica delivered the fruit basket to the wrong room by mistake? Had someone paid Monica to deliver it to the wrong room? She knew that the numbers could have easily been mixed up, but was her mind just playing tricks on her?

"I think there's a crucial question we need to ask, Sarah." Vicky's eyes widened slightly.

"What's that?" Sarah asked.

"If the basket really was delivered to the wrong room, is it possible that Freida wasn't the target at all." Vicky tightened her lips. When she spoke again, her voice was filled with a sense of desolation. "I think we may be looking at a murder, where we don't even know who was the real intended victim."

"You think that someone was trying to kill Roman?" Sarah gasped.

"It sure looks like a possibility."

"Unbelievable. It's horrifying to think that someone used our inn to try and kill someone and potentially killed the wrong person."

"It is, but we have to face it. What happened here happened and there's no getting around it. We have to pin down who was involved in all of this, even if that means stepping on some toes."

"You're right." Sarah yawned. "We'll deal with this in the morning with a clear head. Vicky, be careful, and get some rest okay?"

"I will." Vicky smiled warmly at her sister.

Chapter Fourteen

After Sarah left, Vicky decided to take a walk. She needed to clear her head and calm down after such a tumultuous day. She always did her best thinking in the open air and especially under the stars. She walked away from the inn, towards the plot of land where she and Mitchell were building their house. Of course that would only happen if they didn't lose everything in a lawsuit over Freida's death. She paused at the edge of the foundation that had already been laid. She sat down on it and closed her eyes. When she did she could imagine the house she would share with Mitchell. Not too big, not too small. Just enough room for them, some pets, maybe even some kids. Just enough space to fill with their love.

She thought about the way he had looked at her earlier and had promised to always be in her corner. That meant so much to her, and she reminded herself to thank him for it. They didn't always agree on things, but Mitchell's love for her never seemed to waver.

As her mind shifted back to the murder, she mulled over the possibility that Roman was the target all along. Could Roman have been the intended victim? Could the aim of the poisoning have been to ruin the reputation of the inn and it was done by the same people that sabotaged the banquet hall? She was so engrossed in her thoughts that she nearly jumped out of her skin when she heard footsteps not far from her. Her eyes flew open with fear. She found Mitchell walking towards her.

"Vicky, what are you doing out here?" Mitchell walked across the moon-dappled grass towards her. "I've been trying to reach you." Vicky frowned and pulled out her phone. She saw that she had left it on silent. She had forgotten to turn it back on after creeping after Benny through the banquet hall. She stood up and turned to look at Mitchell. She knew that her face probably told the story of her day.

"I'm sorry. It was on silent." She stared at him for a moment. "I just needed to get away for a few minutes."

Mitchell met her eyes. He stepped closer to her, still holding her gaze with his fierce blue eyes. "Are you all right?" His voice was even as he questioned her, and just a little stern. Vicky knew that he was concerned.

"It's been a long day." She raised her hand to her eyes and covered them as she felt tears well up.

"Oh, sweetheart, none of this is your fault, don't you know that?" Mitchell wrapped his arms around her shoulders and pulled her close against him. "It's a terrible thing that happened, but there was nothing that you could have done to stop it."

"Maybe there was," Vicky mumbled into the curve of his shoulder and neck. "I knew that Freida had been threatened by Roman."

"What?" Mitchell suddenly drew back from her. "Vicky, what are you saying?"

"I'm saying, I heard her telling someone on the phone that she was not afraid of Roman. But I knew she was lying. She was just trying to sound brave." Vicky shook her head. "Maybe if I had insisted that one of them leave, maybe if I had just warned Sarah about it. I don't know, maybe something could have been done."

"Are you truly thinking that Roman Blade is responsible for the murder?" Mitchell's voice wavered with disbelief. "Vicky, do you know the consequences of what you're saying?"

"Not you too." Vicky untangled herself from his arms and refused to look at him. "I know who he is. I know how powerful he is. That doesn't change the fact that he had motive, and opportunity. Does it, Detective?" She turned back to look at Mitchell, her gaze powerful.

"Well, no," Mitchell sputtered as he spoke. "But you can't just go around making accusations with nothing to back them up, no solid proof." He shook his head. Then suddenly he froze. "Did you find some proof?"

"Just that it's possible that the fruit basket was meant for room 301 and it was delivered to room 310 in error." Vicky sighed. "Which is even more confusing, because that may mean that Roman was the target all along."

"Have you told him this?" Mitchell demanded. Vicky looked at him strangely. She wasn't sure why he was staring at her with such urgency.

"No, of course not. We were first going to try and get more information tomorrow. Why?"

"Why?" Mitchell's voice rose. "Vicky, he's running for governor. If there is any chance that there was a threat on his life then you have to tell him. It could be considered an attempted assassination. How could you not tell me this?"

"Mitchell, I didn't think of it that way." Now that she had, Vicky's heart began racing. If Roman had been the target, and Freida only the accidental victim, then would the murderer try again?

"I have to call this in." Mitchell pulled out his cell phone.

"Mitchell wait ... I could be wrong." Vicky looked at him grimly. "We don't know anything for sure yet."

"Even just a suspicion is reason to call it in, Vicky. You know I don't want to put you in a difficult position, but you can't expect me not to follow protocol when it comes to a threat like this."

She knew that Mitchell was right. She couldn't imagine how she would feel, or how Mitchell would feel, if something happened to Roman.

"I know you need to call, Mitchell. You do what you have to do. I'm going to do what I have to do." With that Vicky kissed him quickly and walked off across the grass.

"Vicky, wait!" Mitchell called after her. He already had his phone to his ear. "Where are you going?"

"Don't worry!" Vicky called back. "I'll let you know what I find out."

Vicky was more determined than ever to get to the bottom of things. Within a few minutes she found herself standing outside Ida's door. If anyone could help her uncover the truth, she knew that it would be her Aunt Ida. She knocked lightly on the door. Ida opened it a moment later.

"Vicky, come in." She smiled at her niece. Vicky stepped inside Ida's room. It was the same size as all of the other guest rooms, but it looked a bit smaller because of all the unique souvenirs that Ida had collected from foreign countries over the years. Sometimes the masks could be a little creepy. But the silks, the bright colors draped across the ceiling, were all very soothing to Vicky at that moment.

"Aunt Ida, I want to figure this out tonight. I don't want to wait until tomorrow." Vicky sat down on the edge of her aunt's bed.

"Okay, let's do it." Ida began to pace back and forth in front of the bed. "We know that Freida died because of poisoned berries which did not come from the kitchen, and they were not arranged by the inn even though it was made to look that way. We know that Freida and Roman had a hate-hate relationship. We also know that Freida had created many enemies over the years." She paused and looked over at Vicky. Vicky picked up where she left off.

"We also know that someone went to the trouble of damaging the sprinkler, possibly to damage the reputation of the inn. But, if the two are related that means that someone probably planned this for quite some time." Vicky frowned. "Either with the intent to kill Freida, or the intent to kill Roman."

"How can we solve a murder when we don't even know who the intended victim was?" Ida sighed with exasperation.

"Well, we do know that Freida had some information that was very damaging to Roman's reputation," Vicky reminded her aunt as she stood up. "That makes her the more likely intended victim. Someone would be taking a huge risk if they targeted Roman."

"But if we think that Freida was targeted because of the information she had on Roman, then we have to believe he might have been involved in her murder."

"Aunt Ida, I know that you are fond of him, but a kind man doesn't falsify a war wound, or threaten a reporter," Vicky spoke with determination.

"We don't know for sure that he did any of that. Even if he did, that doesn't make him a murderer. I can't believe that he would do something like this." Ida shook her head and looked at Vicky with displeasure. "You're just buying into the rumors that woman was trying to spread."

"Aunt Ida, that woman was the one who ended up dead." Vicky scowled. "I know it's a terrible thing to think of anyone, but really everything points to him. He had motive, and plenty of opportunity. Maybe he just damaged the sprinkler to throw us off the trail, or the sprinkler had nothing to do with the murder."

"But don't you see? That is why I don't think he had anything to do with it." Ida pursed her lips. "Roman is a very intelligent man, Vicky. He had his mind on an illustrious career, why would he throw all of that away by being so reckless?"

"Are you saying that he is too smart to murder so recklessly?" Vicky asked. She was getting frustrated that her aunt was coming to the defense of a murder suspect.

"I'm saying that if he was trying to protect his political career why would he risk everything by being involved in a scandal like this?" Ida put her hands on her hips. "It just doesn't add up, Vicky. You can't force it to just because you want an easy solution."

Vicky wanted to point out the flaw in her aunt's logic, but the argument she made was a good one. "I guess you're right. He could just as easily have hired someone to take care of the problem. Why would he risk the possibility of casting suspicion on himself by murdering her at the place where he was staying? Why would he get his own hands dirty?" Vicky looked perplexed. "It would be a huge risk to do that. Even if he was trying to satisfy a personal vendetta, I don't think he would choose poison to kill her."

"Exactly!" Ida sighed. "This was not a crime of rage, or passion, this was a premeditated murder. I'm not going to lie, Roman despised Freida, and was even convinced that she was stalking him, but I don't think that would lead him to give her poisonous food and kill her." Ida looked at Vicky. "He isn't flawless, no one is, but I don't think he's that stupid either."

"But that leaves us nowhere!" Vicky's frustration was building more and more by the moment. "If it wasn't Roman that killed Freida, if it was Freida who was the target, then who did it?"

"Maybe another person that Freida wrote a damning article about?" Ida said thoughtfully. "The fruit basket was left at the front desk so anyone could have put the berries in the basket."

"I know, but if we don't figure it out and soon, we might be blamed for this." Vicky could barely keep her mind from spinning. Her thoughts kept returning to the first moment she had laid eyes on Freida's lifeless body. She felt so guilty that the fruit basket that had been delivered to her room, had been what killed her. "You know what, maybe it's time we had a conversation with Roman. Let's see if he knows anything about what happened. It's the best place to start."

"Do you really think that's a good idea?" Ida asked. She looked at Vicky sternly. "He is a powerful man, he won't take it kindly that you are talking to him about the murder and he might not reveal anything, anyway."

"But you've become friends with him."

Ida looked at her with a hint of excitement. "You're right about that. Maybe he would be willing to talk to me."

"So, let's go talk to him now."

"Not us. I will go talk to him. You stay here. I'll let you know how it turns out." She smiled at Vicky. Vicky raised an eyebrow.

"Just how do you intend to get the information out of him, Aunt Ida?" She looked at her aunt nervously.

"Don't you worry about that, Vicky, I will take care of it." Ida picked up one of the orange silks and wrapped it around her from her shoulders to her waist. The silk transformed the simple dress that Ida was wearing into something much more sensual. Vicky watched her aunt leave the room.

Chapter Fifteen

Ida knocked on Roman's door with a light smile on her lips. When he opened the door, he looked a little startled to find her there.

"Ida, it's late. What are you doing out and about?"

"I'm sorry, Roman. Everything that has happened has me quite upset. I thought maybe we could talk." She met his eyes and fluttered her eyelashes lightly.

"Of course, please come in." He stepped back to give her space to enter. Ida moved inside. The room was spotless as she had expected. She walked boldly over to his bed and sat down on the edge of it.

"I'm just so troubled by all of this. The police are saying that Freida died because of the poisonous berries delivered in her fruit basket. The basket was addressed from the inn, but none of us sent it. I'm just so confused."

Roman sat down beside her on the bed. He slid an arm around her shoulders. Ida had to grit her teeth to keep from grabbing his arm and flipping him over her shoulder. She was playing a role, to get the information that she needed.

"Well, I don't know how I can help you," Roman replied with a puzzled expression.

"So, you didn't organize the fruit basket?" Ida asked, immediately realizing that she could have been a bit more subtle when she asked the question.

"Ida, what are you trying to say?" He narrowed his eyes.

"We know that we didn't send the fruit basket and..." Ida stared at him with some fear. She wondered if she had divulged too much information. She was hoping that her instincts about him were correct and that he didn't kill Freida. If he had, he might have good reason to kill her as well.

"What are you saying?" Roman demanded again. He stood up suddenly from the bed and glared at her. "Are you insinuating that I might have given Freida poisonous food?"

"I don't mean to upset you." Ida stood up quickly. "I just wanted to know if you had anything to do with the fruit basket."

"Of course not!" Roman scowled at her. "What you must think of me to even entertain that idea!"

"Please Roman, I'm only trying to find out what happened." Ida looked at him remorsefully.

"No, you're only trying to pin a murder on me!" Roman's voice raised to the point that Ida was startled. "I thought you were far more intelligent than this, Ida. I guess I gave you too much credit!"

Ida glared in return. She knew why he was angry, but she didn't appreciate being insulted.

"I'm doing nothing of the sort. I came here to get the straight story from you!" Ida exclaimed. "I can see that maybe some of the things that Freida wrote about you weren't a lie."

"That woman!" Roman roared. "She has been out to destroy me for years, but no I didn't kill her, and no, I'm not upset that she's dead! How is that for truth, Ida! Now get out of my room!" He pointed to the door. Ida was shocked as she stepped out of the room. She hadn't expected Roman to have such a temper. She also wasn't sure whether he was telling the truth or not. Was his outburst a show to throw her off the truth? Had he truly intended to kill Freida? Ida headed back to her room as quickly as possible. Vicky was waiting for her outside the door.

"What happened?" she asked. She looked at her aunt's stricken expression. "Aunt Ida, he didn't hurt you did he?"

"No. But he's not happy with me. I think I might have said too much." Ida grimaced. "Vicky, let Mitchell handle this. Roman is a bit of a loose cannon."

Vicky stared at her aunt for a long moment. She knew that Ida was edging around the truth. She was instantly angered that Roman would do anything to make her aunt feel awkward. Ida was a strong and vivacious woman and it took a lot to make her feel uncomfortable.

"I'm going to talk to him right now." Vicky started to walk away. Ida grabbed her arm firmly.

"No, Vicky don't. I've upset him enough. He's a powerful man, and I shouldn't have made such a serious suggestion. Wait until the morning, when we might get more information from the grocery store about who ordered the fruit basket. Mitchell can question Roman. It really isn't a good idea for us to pursue this on our own." Ida squeezed Vicky's arm. "Leave this alone for tonight."

Vicky recalled hearing a similar speech from Mitchell not that long before. She decided not to argue with her aunt.

"You're right. In the morning we'll find out more. Then we'll know what really happened." Vicky glanced towards her apartment. "I'm going to head in for the night."

"Me too," Ida nodded. After Ida disappeared inside her room, Vicky began to fume. She was certain that Roman had done something to frighten her aunt. Even if he wasn't a murderer, Vicky needed to speak to him. She lingered by Ida's door for a few moments. She knew that Mitchell wasn't home. He was more than likely busy setting up a protective detail for Roman. Which meant that Vicky would only have one chance to question Roman alone and see if she could get the truth out of him, and try to convince him not to cause the inn trouble and that was exactly what she was going to do.

Chapter Sixteen

Once Vicky was sure that Ida wasn't listening at the door, she began walking down the hallway towards Roman's room. It was deserted at the moment.

Vicky was relieved that no one would spot her heading for Roman's door. She made her way down the hallway and around the corner. With every step she took she grew more irate. She knew that she should try to diffuse the situation for the sake of the inn's future even though she hated the thought that anyone would do anything to upset her aunt. The door to Roman's room was closed. However, when she neared it, she heard the sound of a scuffle inside. She pressed her ear against the door and listened for a moment.

"Let go of me!" Roman's voice boomed from inside the room. It made Vicky's body grow tense. Who was he yelling at?

"You won't do what it takes to win. You don't care if you win and I can't take it anymore. I don't want to be on a losing team. We won't lose if you're dead." The voice carried through the door and seized Vicky's heart with fear. She recognized the voice. It was Trevor. She was almost certain of it. She grabbed the knob of the door and twisted it. The knob turned, but the door wouldn't budge. Was Trevor trying to get revenge for Freida's death? Had Roman admitted the truth to him?

"You don't have to do this, we can still win. You've lost your mind. You're going to ruin everything. You'd be throwing the campaign away. You will be throwing your future away. Our future. We can just pretend none of this ever happened." Vicky recognized the fear in Roman's voice.

Her heart began pounding hard. She shoved her shoulder against the door. She could tell from the light give that there was furniture in the way of the door.

Inside she could hear the struggle continuing. There was grunting, cursing, and even some sounds of skin colliding against skin.

"I never lose, Roman. But you won't do what it takes to win," Trevor's voice raised. "Winning is everything. I needed you to take this seriously. The only answer is to kill you." Vicky heard a loud crash as if perhaps a lamp had been knocked over. She slammed her shoulder against the door. It finally moved enough for her to squeeze through it. On the other side she saw Roman pinned against the wall by Trevor. Trevor had his hands around Roman's throat. Vicky didn't have time to think about caution. She rushed forward and grabbed Trevor by the shoulders. She tried to tug him away from Roman.

"No!" Trevor screamed. "He has to die! He is a coward! He doesn't deserve to win. I did everything to help him and he blames me for Freida's death. He won't do what's necessary!"

Vicky's heart slammed against her chest. She dug her fingernails into the sides of Trevor's neck. When Trevor felt the pain, he tried to wriggle out of her grasp. Vicky only dug her nails in deeper.

"Let him go!" Vicky growled. Roman's face was turning a deep shade of purple. He struggled to take a breath. Trevor finally released him in order to reach up and grab Vicky's hands by the wrists. Roman slumped to the floor, gasping for air. Trevor spun her around in front of him. In that moment she saw his crazed eyes and her body filled with fear. He landed his knee into her stomach. Vicky doubled over at the pain in her stomach. She stumbled back a few steps.

Trevor saw the opportunity and struck her hard in the face. Vicky fell across the bed, stunned by the pain that flooded her jaw. She was about to stand up when Trevor punched her again. Her mind spun as she tried to work out what was happening. Why would he want to kill Roman?

"Stay down, Vicky," he warned her. "I've already killed once, I intend to kill Roman, too. I'd really like to avoid killing you. If only Roman had eaten the berries none of this would have happened!"

Vicky was terrified by his words. She knew she had rushed into a dangerous situation that she might not be able to get out of without some help. Worse than that, Roman was crumpled on the floor. She wasn't sure if he had passed out or if he was dead. He was not going to be able to come to her defense and no one else knew that she had even come into his room. She had to think of a way to escape and fast.

Trevor tore down one of the curtains and used it to tie Vicky's hands behind her back. He tied the knots so tightly that Vicky could barely move her wrists. She started to feel an even deeper panic build within her. Satisfied that Vicky was sufficiently restrained Trevor turned back to Roman. He glared down at the man on the floor.

"Weak, that's all you are, I did everything for you. Do you really think you can play dead you fool?" Trevor swung a foot hard into Roman's side. Roman cried out in pain and curled up in an attempt to protect the more vulnerable areas of his body. Vicky was relieved that he was alive, but she knew that he wouldn't be for long. Trevor was already ready to kick him again.

"Trevor! Why did you kill Freida?" Vicky asked. She wanted to distract him, but she also wanted to know the truth. She needed to do something, anything, to keep him from killing Roman. Trevor paused and turned back to face her.

"I didn't mean to kill her." He stared at her for a moment. "The berries were never meant for Freida they were meant for Roman, but that idiot delivered the fruit basket to the wrong room."

"But why would you want to kill Roman?"

"I didn't really. When I was out walking and I recognized some poisonous berries from one of my books on botany, I knew I had the perfect way to win the election."

"How?" Vicky asked.

"By making Roman sick. I did more research and I knew that the quantity of berries I put in the basket wouldn't kill him it would just make him sick. But as the evidence shows the quantity would be lethal for someone of Freida's build. I never meant to kill anyone I just wanted Roman to get sick."

"But why?" Vicky asked incredulously.

"So we would win, obviously." Vicky noticed that Trevor was getting more and more agitated. His hands were twitching at his sides. "It was the perfect way to get the sympathy vote. An attempted assassination. Then Roman had a greater chance of winning."

"You murdered someone so Roman could win?"

"It isn't my fault that Freida is dead!" He stared at her. "That was never my intention. Really the inn is to blame. If the basket was delivered to the right room, then no one would be dead and Roman would be in a better position of winning. But Roman thinks I've taken things too far. He doesn't understand that I would prefer that he was dead than we lose the campaign."

Vicky's eyes widened, the man was clearly crazy. "Did you break the sprinkler in the banquet hall?" Vicky tried to think of anything to say that would delay the inevitable.

"That was a complete waste of time." His voice rose and his fingers twitched faster at his sides with agitation. "When Sarah took me for a tour I saw that the restaurant was closed for painting. She explained that dinner would be served in the banquet hall. Roman and I were meant to have a dinner meeting to finalize some scheduling. So I decided to flood the banquet hall so I would have room service for dinner with Roman. Then I could poison Roman's food with the berries as it would have been much easier to add the berries in the room than in the restaurant. Then bad weather was forecast, which was an added bonus."

"But he didn't order room service."

"I know, once again he wasn't prepared to do what was necessary to win. He didn't want to do the work. He said that he didn't want to have the meeting, he wanted to have a relaxing dinner. He wanted to eat outside and enjoy the scenery. So, when that fell through I thought I would use them in a fruit basket delivered from management as an apology, but then everything went wrong when it was delivered to the wrong room. I also wanted to plant some berries in the kitchen so it looked like the berries came from the kitchen. That way the police would have somewhere to focus that was pointed far away from me. But every time I went down there the chef or a staff member was in there. So I thought if I broke the sprinkler head the staff would be distracted and I could plant the berries."

"But we didn't find any berries in the kitchen."

"I know. I couldn't plant them. It was a complete waste of time. When I went to put them in the kitchen all of the staff had left the kitchen, but there was a delivery driver there so I couldn't leave any berries there. All of that trouble for nothing. The note on the card pointing the police in the inn's direction helped a bit I guess. But then the basket was delivered to the wrong room. I would have delivered it to Roman myself, but I thought it would point suspicion directly at me."

"Why did you want to ruin the inn's reputation?" Vicky asked.

"I never wanted to," he said. "It was a necessary consequence for my plan to work."

"Trevor." Vicky shook her head with disgust. Out of the corner of her eye she could see that Roman was still on the floor. "You have murdered someone to win an election. It's crazy!"

"No, it's essential!" Trevor said with determination. "There is no point in entering if you don't win. Roman had all of these resources and connections to help him win, but that's not enough. You can't just sit back and hope, you have to take control. And that is what I'm going to do, I'm going to get rid of the problem. If Roman is dead he can't lose, can he? If you're dead you can't tell everyone what I did, can you?"

"But there are other ways, Trevor! Please, be reasonable." Vicky stared into is crazed eyes.

"Don't do this, Trevor. There's still time for you to get help. You can still save yourself."

"See? That's the problem. Everyone is so selfish. I don't care what happens to me, Vicky. I did this for Roman. And does he thank me for it? No!" Trevor shook his head with exasperation. He turned back towards Vicky. "I never meant for you or anyone else to get hurt in any of this. But I can't let you live."

He raised his hands and reached for Vicky's throat. Vicky tried to roll away, but he was too fast for her. She felt his strong hands curve around her neck and the air begin to be cut off from her lungs. Just when she thought there was no chance that she was getting out of the room alive, she heard pounding on the door. Suddenly, the door burst open. The furniture that had been blocking it went flying. Ida flipped into the room, and landed directly behind Trevor. She didn't hesitate to grab him by the shoulder and the crook of his elbow. She flung him easily over her hip and across the room.

"Aunt Ida!" Vicky gasped. Ida winked once at Vicky and then pounced on top of Trevor who was trying to get to his feet. She pinned him down with her knee, then pulled his arms behind his back.

"I guess you'll be needing these." Mitchell climbed over the debris of the furniture holding a pair of handcuffs. He handed them to Ida, who was more than a little surprised that he would trust her with them. Mitchell rushed to Vicky's side and untied her.

"Are you hurt?" He looked at her with desperation in his eyes. "Did he hurt you?" She could see the fury building in his gaze.

"No, check on Roman," Vicky insisted. "Make sure he's okay." Mitchell turned to see Roman slowly sitting up from the floor. He looked like he had been put through quite a beating, and his face was still off color from the attempted strangulation. Mitchell immediately called for an ambulance and back-up. Once Ida had Trevor in handcuffs, Mitchell read him his rights. But his gaze never left Vicky. She was bruised from the attack. Ida wrapped an arm around her shoulders.

"Aunt Ida, how did you know?" Vicky looked at her aunt with disbelief. "If you hadn't come in when you did, I wouldn't have made it."

"Don't say that! Don't even think it!" Ida looked into her niece's eyes. "I didn't know." Ida shook her head. "I decided that I better come back and talk to Roman again, before he could cause the inn and all of us some major trouble, and that's when I heard what was happening."

Vicky looked at her aunt with fondness. They both had had the same thought, and Vicky was very lucky that they had, because Trevor had easily overpowered her. If her aunt hadn't arrived when she did, Vicky might never have made it out of the room alive. She shuddered at the thought. Ida pulled her closer.

Vicky stared at Trevor handcuffed on the floor. The entire time he had been right under her nose. It made her very unsettled to think that she had suspected the very man who had been the target of Trevor's attack. Not to mention the fact that she got Monica to deliver the basket to Freida's room, a fruit basket that killed her. Mitchell helped Roman to his feet.

"Are you okay?" Mitchell looked Roman over to be sure that he wasn't seriously injured.

"I think so," Roman's voice was rough. He reached up and rubbed at his neck. "Thanks to these two brave women." He looked over at Ida and Vicky with gratitude.

Mitchell glanced over at Ida and Vicky, then he looked back at Roman. "I have an ambulance on the way."

"Thank you," Roman said.

Mitchell turned away from Roman and walked over to Vicky. Vicky looked up at him with some concern. She knew that he might be furious that she had put herself in such a dangerous position, that she had not let him know what she was up to. Mitchell's expression was quite serious as he looked down into her eyes.

"Are you okay?" he asked. His voice was barely above a whisper. Vicky nodded and opened her arms to him. Mitchell embraced her. He held her gently against him. "I love you, Vicky."

"I love you, too," Vicky murmured. She felt comforted by his warmth. All of the pain she was experiencing seemed minor compared to the wave of love that washed over her.

Chapter Seventeen

Once Trevor was in custody, and Roman had been evaluated at the hospital, Vicky and Sarah met in the kitchen. Henry prepared them a pot of very strong coffee.

"I can't believe that all of this was over politics," Sarah said sadly. "Now Roman has dropped out of the campaign, and Trevor will have no chance of being the campaign manager for a winning candidate."

"Well, to be fair it was more about one very disillusioned, crazy man that would try anything to win. Still, it makes my heart ache to think that Freida died because of this." Vicky shook her head. "Apparently, Roman had no idea that Trevor tried to poison him to make it look like an assassination attempt. The lengths people will go to in order to win. What a terrible thing to think that someone died because of a political campaign."

"I think it was an eye-opening experience for Roman," Sarah spoke quietly. "He even admitted that the injury he claimed was a war injury wasn't one at all. He says that he is turning over a new leaf of honesty. Maybe when he recovers from all of this he will run for office again."

"Maybe," Vicky agreed. "Putting yourself out there in the public eye really does make you vulnerable to people who could target you. But you would never expect the threat to be in your own campaign committee. I never would have thought Trevor was capable of something like that."

"He is very deluded." Henry set down two mugs of coffee in front of them.

"To think he went so far as to damage the sprinkler to try and plant the berries and to try to get Roman to have room service. What an elaborate plan," Sarah said. She stared down at her coffee. "I honestly thought we were going to lose everything." She looked up at Vicky. "If it weren't for you, Vicky, I think I would have lost my mind."

"Sarah, we're a team." Vicky smiled warmly at her sister. "If it weren't for you, I wouldn't be living the amazing life I am now. We have to look out for each other."

"That's the truth." Sarah raised her mug of coffee. Vicky raised hers as well. "Here's to the Heavenly Highland Inn, and many more years of keeping each other sane."

"I will definitely drink to that." Vicky laughed. As the coffee mugs clinked, Henry chuckled.

"Now get out of my kitchen, I have delicious food to prepare!"

The End

More Cozy Mysteries by Cindy BelL

Heavenly Highland Inn Cozy Mysteries

Murdering the Roses

Dead in the Daisies

Killing the Carnations

Drowning the Daffodils

Suffocating the Sunflowers

Books, Bullets and Blooms

A Deadly Serious Gardening Contest

A Bridal Bouquet and a Body

Sage Gardens Cozy Mysteries

Birthdays Can Be Deadly

Money Can Be Deadly

Trust Can Be Deadly

Ties Can Be Deadly

Rocks Can Be Deadly

Numbers Can Be Deadly

Chocolate Centered Cozy Mysteries

The Sweet Smell of Murder

A Deadly Delicious Delivery

A Treacherous Tasty Trail

Luscious Pastry at a Lethal Party

Dune House Cozy Mysteries

Seaside Secrets

Boats and Bad Guys

Treasured History

Hidden Hideaways

Dodgy Dealings

Suspects and Surprises

Wendy the Wedding Planner Cozy Mysteries

Matrimony, Money and Murder

Chefs, Ceremonies and Crimes

Knives and Nuptials

Mice, Marriage and Murder

Bekki the Beautician Cozy Mysteries

Hairspray and Homicide

A Dyed Blonde and a Dead Body

Mascara and Murder

Pageant and Poison

Conditioner and a Corpse

Mistletoe, Makeup and Murder

Hairpin, Hair Dryer and Homicide

Blush, a Bride and a Body

Shampoo and a Stiff

Cosmetics, a Cruise and a Killer

Lipstick, a Long Iron and Lifeless

Camping, Concealer and Criminals

Treated and Dyed

Printed in Great Britain
by Amazon